THE
MISCHIEVOUS
SPINSTER

THE MISCHIEVOUS SPINSTER

== Marian Lorraine ==

WALKER AND COMPANY
NEW YORK

First published in the United States of America
in 1983 by the Walker Publishing Company, Inc.

Published simultaneously in Canada by John Wiley & Sons
Canada, Limited, Rexdale, Ontario.

ISBN: 0-8027-0726-2

Library of Congress Catalog Card Number: 82-62787

Printed in the United States of America

10   9   8   7   6   5   4   3   2   1

==1==

TEMPTED OUTDOORS BY the gentle breezes and warm sun this lovely day in the first week of June, two fashionable young women took time out from their packing to sit for a few minutes in the small garden leading off the dining room of the town house.

"Well, Julia," said the older one, so recognized not as much by her personal appearance, for she was lovely of face and form and could have been taken for a young girl, as by a subtle aura of self-assurance and a certain casual flair in her toilette, "one more Season behind us. But *this* time we won't go home empty-handed."

The younger girl looked at her sister's mischievous expression and broke into delighted laughter. "Tonia, you are the most outrageous girl. How dare you say such a thing?"

"Colin *is* going with us, isn't he?" Antonia asked with a contrived innocence, still indulging her irrepressible sense of fun.

With a beatific smile Julia vowed, "Tonia, I am so happy!"

"Yes, darling, I know. And I am very happy for you. I adore Colin myself. My nose is quite out of joint that you have been so lucky as to find your love when I, though having been out for years longer, am still looking for mine."

"That is a hum, and you know it, Tonia. You are not looking. You have turned away more suitors than you can count."

"But that only means that my Prince Charming has yet to come on his white charger," Antonia said whimsically. "And do not tell me that I am much too particular, for you were well along to being considered on the shelf yourself before Colin came into your life."

"Yes, that is true," Julia conceded with a giggle. "We were becoming known as the 'Radcliffe spinsters'!"

"Well, at least one of us has flummoxed the tattlemongers," Tonia gloated. "We had better get back to work. When is Colin coming today?"

"About two. He has some arrangements to make this morning, also. I can't *wait* until we go home to introduce him to Mama and Papa."

"Mama has written that she is sure she would recognize him on sight from having been apprized of every element of his countenance and superior character," Tonia teased.

"Well, he *is* perfect," Julia retorted in defense. "You have said so yourself."

Sharing an understanding look, both girls laughed and went back into the house. Upstairs, they left the connecting doors between their rooms open so they might converse and traffic back and forth.

"Tonia, I can't believe we bought all these gowns. Some I haven't even worn. I should never have let you corrupt me. You are shockingly extravagant."

"I'm afraid you are right, love. I just can't seem to resist beautiful clothes. But we will likely have use of them all when we accompany Colin to his family's home, so I will not allow that we were imprudent," Tonia denied impenitently.

As Julia busied herself with packing her toiletry items, she felt a faint pang of apprehension. She *could* wish that Colin's family had been in London. It would be so much more satisfying to know that she had met their approval. Seeking encouragement from her redoubtable sister, she ventured hesitantly, "Tonia, I have been wondering these last few days about how Colin's mother and brother will receive me. Our station does not at all compare with theirs, and I expect they had hopes of him being better connected."

Surprised by this unexpected show of diffidence, Antonia looked at her sharply. "I hope you are not going to allow yourself to be intimidated, Julia. You always have your head on your shoulders and possess such a calm disposition that I would not have expected you to seem so poor-spirited."

2

"You know I am not, Tonia. It's just that it would be so much more pleasant if his family would give us their blessing," Julia said wistfully.

"Well, I do think you are living in a fool's paradise if you expect clear sailing, my love," her sister remarked bluntly. "It is true that I have never met the duke, as he seems to have rather an antipathy to London society, so I really cannot judge from what I have heard of him, though we must take some measure of comfort in that Colin seems to be on very good terms with him. As for Colin's mother—well, *there* you have your work cut out for you! I *have* met *her,* though it was several years ago, and she definitely attaches a great deal of importance to rank. After Colin's father died, the *on dit* had it that she kept the Earl of Merrill dangling for two years because she could not bear to relinquish the title of duchess."

"But she did marry him," Julia said hopefully.

"Yes. In the end she could not refuse, for it was a love match, and the earl is said to be able to handle her beautifully. While she may be persuadable, I doubt she will welcome you with open arms."

"I suspect Colin is anticipating some opposition, too," Julia noted ruefully. "He has made a special point of assuring me that I am the most important thing in his life and that nothing could ever change that."

"You do believe him, don't you?" Tonia asked.

"Yes, of course. I know he would not permit anything to come between us. But I would feel badly if our marriage alienated him from his family."

"Julia, I insist that you stop looking for trouble. It is not as though we don't have illustrious connections. We just happen to be of a younger branch of the family. Our ancestry need not be considered exceptionable. And Papa is not exactly a nobody, you know. His textbooks have wide distribution and are admired by the most discerning scholars. So I will thank you to hold up your head. If Colin could hear you express these doubts, he would turn you over his knee."

"The thing of it is, Tonia, I don't *really* have any doubts. It's just that I think perhaps I ought to."

"You are a little goose, Julia. You should accept your good fortune for what it is and fight to keep and enjoy it," her sister scolded.

Julia smiled at her sister with affection. "Thank you, Tonia," she told her gratefully. "I only needed to have someone else confirm my own convictions. For myself I am not concerned. It's only that I care so much for Colin…"

"You need not worry about Colin, darling. That young man has a great deal of backbone. You may be sure he will weather the storm. Besides, can you really imagine that anyone who knows and loves him could possibly disown him?"

"Well, there is *that*," Julia allowed, glad to have her foolish fears allayed.

Having satisfied themselves that everything was being properly carried out, they left the two young servants to finish packing, directing their maid to make sure nothing was forgotten. Then they went down to the morning room to call for a light lunch, and were soon enjoying an omelette with bacon and toast.

"Where did Aunt Margot go this morning?" Julia asked.

"She was promised to Lady Sam for an early shopping excursion, and you know *that* would make shift of most of the day," Tonia replied.

They sat quietly for a few moments, drinking their coffee, each with her own particular memories of this unexpectedly eventful Season. Presently Julia decided, "I had better go to change before Colin arrives. Will you drive with us?"

"Not today, thank you. I really am expecting Aunt Margot to return at a reasonable hour, and I would like to spend a little time with her, since we leave early tomorrow."

An hour later the knocker sounded, just as Tonia was about to enter the library, so she came back to greet a favoured guest.

"Hello, Colin. What a beautiful day for a drive," she said gaily.

The pair presented an incongruous appearance, for Tonia was

4

only two inches over five feet, and her future brother-in-law towered over her by more than a foot. He was an impressive looking young man, with blond hair, a pleasant face, steady blue eyes, a firm chin, broad shoulders and a trim, well-muscled figure.

"Come with us, Tonia," he coaxed amiably.

"Thank you, Colin. I am tempted, but I have some last minute things to take care of. Come upstairs to wait. I will tell Julia you're here."

With a happy glow Julia hurried to greet her betrothed. When she entered the drawing room, she was instantly embraced and soundly kissed.

"I missed our morning ride, Julia, darling. I am looking forward to the day when I can see you first thing even when I have an early appointment," Colin murmured in her ear.

She smiled, saying softly, "That sounds lovely, Colin."

He kissed her again, then possessively tucked her arm through his as he told her, "I asked Tonia to come with us, but she refused."

"She is waiting for Aunt Margot. If you wouldn't mind, I would like to join them in a little while."

"We'll just drive for an hour or so," he agreed affably.

Left to her own pursuits, Tonia situated herself at the writing table in the library with the purpose of settling her accounts, closing her mind to the exorbitant sums she was obliged to pay. Both she and Julia had substantial fortunes in their own right, inheritances from two maiden great-aunts to whom they had been very much attached and by whom they were well loved in return, so they had never felt a need to practice economy. Consequently they rarely did so, though it must be said that Tonia was more the spendthrift, while Julia merely followed her lead, not having quite the passion for elegance that her sister did. Just as Tonia was finishing, the door opened and two very handsome, fashionable ladies entered, looking a trifle weary.

"Well, I can see that you have spent a scrambling day," Tonia commented. "Come sit down, and we will have tea. Did you find anything you couldn't resist?"

"We were shopping for the children," Lady Samantha Barkley replied. "Wait until you see the enchanting dresses and nankeens we bought for the little ones. And playthings, too, of course. They always expect something when we go to them from London."

Tonia laughed indulgently. "I can just imagine the two of you testing all the toys. I don't doubt you had a famous time."

"And so we did," her aunt told her pertly. "You should have been with us."

The tea arrived, and Tonia poured, handing each lady a steaming cup. As they relaxed and sipped slowly, Lady Samantha eyed Tonia speculatively. "Well, my dear, are you leaving your usual quota of broken hearts?"

"Lady Sam! You make me sound like a *femme fatale,*" Tonia protested with an aggrieved expression.

"You are not going to tell me that there were not several gentlemen with dashed hopes, are you? Won't wash, Tonia. The *on dit* has it otherwise."

"Well, that is not precisely the same thing as broken hearts," the girl claimed in defense. "And, as usual, it will be a case of out of sight, out of mind."

"Not in every case, Antonia," Lady Margot, the widow of the late Baron Walton, refuted. "You have at least three faithful swains who are waiting in the wings if ever you should decide to settle down."

"I am beginning to doubt I ever shall," her niece remarked. "I am come to enjoy my independence, and I haven't seen anything I would wish to trade it for." She reached up to secure a fallen strand, and Lady Samantha asked, "Tonia, how do you keep that absurd *coiffure* in place? Considering the nicety of the rest of your toilette, it has always confounded me that you wear your hair in that totally disordered fashion."

"Don't be misled, my friend," Lady Margot advised. "She knows very well what she is about. The style is uncommonly distinctive. And I am persuaded the gentlemen find it extremely

6

seductive and have fantasies about removing one strategic pin to see the mass tumble down her back."

"Aunt Margot, that is utterly ridiculous!" Tonia protested with a giggle.

The door opened then, and Julia entered with her betrothed. "I hoped you would be here, Lady Sam," she exclaimed. "I wanted to see you before we all left town."

"Hello, Julia, darling. Have you set a date for your wedding?"

"We have been thinking about the last week in September."

"That should give you time," the lady remarked cryptically. "Have you written to your mother, Lord Neville?"

"Yes, though I don't know when my letter will catch up with her."

"How much longer are she and the earl staying on the Continent? They have been gone for almost a year."

"Yes, well, after Waterloo, they and some of the others who had been waiting out the war in Brussels decided to take the Grand Tour now that things were quiet. They were in Italy for the winter and then left for Spain to spend a month or two before returning to Paris, where I expect they could be now. I sent a letter to their friends there. Mother will hear the news before she comes home, I'm sure."

"A wise move on your part, my boy," Lady Margot noted.

Colin laughed and acknowledged, "Yes, I expect there will be something of a turn-up, given my mother's tendency to fly up in the boughs unreasonably. But when she realizes how much I love Julia, she will come round. And then when she takes time to know her, she will understand and be happy for us both."

The young man's confidence was not shared by at least two of the company, but they tactfully refrained from voicing their skepticism. Instead Lady Samantha asked, "What of the duke? Have you told him?"

"No, I don't know precisely where Derek is now, though Aunt Alvinia has written that he plans to return to the castle in July. So we will likely arrive there before him. I don't expect any objections from him, however," Colin added to satisfy the older women's curiosity. "He will be happy to see me settle down. He said as much when I last saw him in March, before I came to town."

"And he expects you to continue the line?" Lady Margot asked, causing Julia to blush at the indelicacy.

"It appears so, though he is only thirty-five and so hardly out of the running himself," Colin said, taking Julia's hand in his.

"Well, I don't doubt you are going to have an interesting summer," Lady Samantha said as she rose to leave. "Do keep me apprised of all the developments."

They all laughed as her friend accused her of being a nosy old busybody. Colin offered to drive her home, reminding Julia that he would return in time to escort her to the theatre.

When they had gone, Lady Margot turned to her younger niece. "My dear, I am so pleased that you have found such an admirable young man. You are extremely fortunate—as he is himself."

"Thank you, Aunt Margot. But I have the impression that you and Lady Sam do not think our news will be well received."

"I may be wrong, Julia. And Carla does dote on Colin. I don't doubt he has reason to expect her acceptance. Do not worry about it. He will handle the situation," Lady Margot said, leaning over to pat her niece's hand.

"I wish it would be otherwise," Julia said with a sigh. "But I suppose it is best to know what to expect. I am glad you're going with me, Tonia."

"And I, my dear, am looking forward to the experience," her sister replied with an expectant light in her eye. "Things have been going along so smoothly these past several years that it will be a welcome change to have an opportunity to beard a lion and lioness in their den."

"Heaven help the lion and lioness," Lady Margot remarked expressively, raising her eyes and provoking them all to laughter.

"Oh, you two could stage a play with your nonsense," Julia declared, wiping her eyes. "I must go change for the evening. Are you going out, Tonia?"

"No. I closed the books today. My Season is over. I want to retire early. Run along. I'll waken you in plenty of time tomorrow. Tell Colin not to be late. It will be a long day."

With this admonishment, Tonia went to her own room, prepared to spend a solitary evening. Her aunt had an engagement to attend a card party, which meant she would likely not get home until after midnight. Still, Lady Margot had promised to rise early to see the two girls off on their journey.

As she lounged comfortably on the luxurious, champagne-coloured velvet chaise, making occasional notes to remind herself of last minute things to be done, Tonia felt a peculiar sense of anticipation. There was really no accounting for it, unless it could be due to Julia's interesting new situation. Tonia began to wonder about the duke. Because of his consequence, his name often was brought up in conversation. But until Colin entered the picture, she had not given his older brother a second thought. It was strange that he never appeared at any of the fashionable affairs and had avoided being entrapped by some ambitious lady. Though there *was* one rumour a few years ago, Tonia remembered now, that Cecily Mervyn, the widow of the old Earl of Falmouth, had some sort of claim on him. However, nothing had come of it. She was still unattached and very much a personage in the *ton,* a lovely blonde of only twenty-seven years. Not without cause, she seemed to harbour a faint animosity towards Tonia, as did several other young women who could not appreciate the elder Miss Radcliffe's perennial popularity with the male element. Gentlemen generally found Tonia's appearance, lively personality and wit very much to their taste. Because this natural capacity to charm persisted year after year—Tonia had made her debut almost a dozen years ago and now had reached the advanced age of twenty-nine—the green-eyed females had long ago spent their tolerance, if indeed they had ever had any at all. Not that Tonia lacked female friends. Those who did not regard her as a threat liked her very well, for she could always be depended upon to enliven the company.

She retired early, stirring slightly when Julia came in, and in the morning wakened in a buoyant mood. She looked forward to going home, as she did every year after a hectic Season. For years she had taken lessons in painting and now had developed into a notable artist in her own right. In London she put aside this interest. But in the country she spent many hours at her easel. And she particularly liked to pursue this pastime in the summer months when the light was good and the days were long. She busied herself with last minute packing and then knocked on the door to waken Julia.

"I'm up, Tonia. I couldn't sleep. From the excitement of going home, I expect." The door opened and a bright-eyed, fully-dressed young lady linked arms with her sister and said, "Let's go down to eat. I'm famished. We didn't go to supper after the theater—it was too late. Aunt Margot came in just as we did and reminded me to waken her. But I do hate to disturb her so early."

"She would be very much put out if we didn't," Tonia remarked. "Besides, she is unbelievably resilient. It won't faze her in the least." So saying, she marched to her aunt's door and called out, "Aunt Margot, Julia and I are going down to breakfast. It is early, so you need not hurry."

"Thank you, Tonia," a sleepy voice anwered. "I'll join you in a few minutes."

True to her word, Lady Margot appeared in the morning room before the girls were half finished. She was dressed in a flowing, filmy wrapper, and her hair was in some disarray, but she made a charming picture and seemed not a bit dismayed at being roused at such an unfashionable hour.

"Well, my dears, once again we must go our different ways. It will not be the same next year," she noted regretfully, "now that Julia is to be married. Not that I do not wish you happy, darling," she added hastily. "It's just that I always enjoy having your company during the Season. I must say there is something to be said for not rushing into matrimony. You both have had several good years on the town."

"Aunt Margot, that is rather an inelegant way of stating the case," Tonia accused with a giggle. "It sounds positively indecent."

"And so it is as far as you are concerned, you shameless girl. Someday you are going to meet your match."

"Is that a promise?" Tonia asked impishly. "I'm not a confirmed spinster, you know."

"What you are is an incurable mischief," her aunt told her.

"Aunt Margot," Julia interrupted, feeling suddenly nostalgic, now realizing that many things would change, "Thank you so much for having us with you all these years. Our stays in London have always been so comfortable, and you are a darling to be such an accommodating hostess."

"Nonsense, Julia. It pleases me to have you, as you well know. My own daughter has been a sorry disappointment to me."

"Aunt Margot, you know that is not so!" Tonia chided. "You dote on your grandchildren."

"Oh, I don't mean in *that* way. Valerie has performed that role very well. But that's part of the problem. Ever since she married eight years ago, she has done *nothing* but increase and at twenty-eight has already descended into being a dull, self-satisfied matron," Lady Margot complained. "I have never once been able to persuade her to join us in Town."

"She is happy with her home and family," Tonia admonished. "We are not all the same."

"No," her aunt said with a sigh, "you're right, of course. And now I must tell you what Samantha and I have planned. After Julia's wedding, we have decided to go to the United States to see our other grandchildren."

"How exciting!" Julia exclaimed. "But," she added dubiously, as the daring of it struck her, "it is such a long journey, with nothing to see but water for weeks and weeks!"

"Not if you are lucky enough to have favourable winds," Lady Margot said. "John writes that the American schooners are very fast and rarely take more than a month."

"You and Lady Sam will have a famous time, Aunt Margot,"

Tonia said with an affectionate smile. "Next time I will go with you. However, now we must make ready for a less exotic trip. What time is Colin coming, Julia?"

"Half-past eight. We had better hurry. Colin will not want to keep the horses standing."

When Colin arrived, he was dismayed by the amount of baggage to be loaded and understood why Tonia had insisted that they hire an extra carriage to travel with them.

"Good Lord! It looks like enough for an army."

Julia blushed, but Tonia only said airily, "We always over-indulge our fancies when we come to Town. You must become accustomed."

"Tonia! You will have Colin thinking I am pound-foolish!" Julia protested.

"No, no, I will not. I confess I am the culprit, Colin," Tonia said, cheerfully taking the blame.

At last all was in readiness, and the three took their leave from Lady Margot amidst many promises and words of caution. With one last embrace all around, the young man helped his charges into the travelling carriage, directing the coachman to give the horses their heads, and soon they were tooling along at a brisk pace, heading for Bedfordshire.

2

THEIR DESTINATION WAS only some fifty miles distant, as the Radcliffe home was located a mile or so beyond the old historic town of Dunstable, chosen by the scholarly Mr. Radcliffe for its easy access to Oxford, Cambridge and London, all of which were important sources of research for his works. Still, in a travelling chaise the journey would take most of the day. So the travellers settled back to relax and enjoy themselves in easy conversation as the carriage rumbled along, out-distancing the second, heavily-laden vehicle which lumbered behind at a slower pace. They were to come together again at St. Albans, where the party planned to stop for lunch and do some exploring to stretch their muscles.

A little after one o'clock they pulled up at the end of Abbey Mill Lane in front of the Fighting Cocks Inn, reputedly one of the oldest inns in England.

They entered the small inn to refresh themselves and then bespoke a picnic lunch to eat outdoors along the banks of the river. It was a lovely peaceful day, and all three decided they were much too lazy to play the tourist, satisfying themselves with a cursory look at the cathedral, which had been built around the shrine of the martyred St. Alban.

"Tell us something of the elusive duke, Colin," Tonia requested when they had returned to the carriage and were comfortably settled for the next stage of the journey. "Is he at all like you, I wonder?"

Colin burst out laughing. "My God! Wouldn't he be astounded by *that* notion. My brother, my dear Tonia, is a character unto himself. I know no one like him."

"Oh dear! You have quite dashed my hopes," Tonia mourned. "I had already pictured him as an older version of yourself and decided that we should suit beautifully."

Julia giggled. "Tonia, you are absurd," she chided.

"I thought it was a lovely idea," the lady pursued undaunted. "I imagined us one big happy family. But I see it is not to be, for I don't mean to settle for less. Really, my dear boy," she said, "you have with one stroke put me to grass."

"Tonia, never in my life have I known such a mischief," Colin said with a hearty laugh. "And if you mean to pull your tricks on Derek, I must warn you, you do so at your own risk. He is not easily gulled."

Tonia grinned impishly, showing the deep dimples that so fascinated the gentlemen. "Well, *that* sounds interesting. Do not tell me more. I shall delight in my delusions. At least until I have met the Incomparable Duke."

Presently they slowed down to pass through the town of Dunstable. Two miles farther on, they turned off the road to follow a drive leading to a moderate-sized manor house. They stopped under a *porte-cochère* that had been added recently for the convenience of passengers, and Colin descended from the carriage to help the ladies down the steps.

Their arrival had been remarked eagerly, and the master and mistress of the manor were on hand to greet them.

"My dears," the lady exclaimed, embracing both her daughters at once, "it has seemed so long this time."

"That is probably because you have been impatient to meet Julia's young man," Tonia teased as she stepped aside to allow her sister to draw Colin forward.

"Colin, I am pleased to present you to my mother and father," Julia said proudly. "Mama and Papa—Lord Colin Neville."

The gentlemen clasped hands, and Colin bowed to Mrs. Radcliffe, saying, "I am amazed, ma'am. No one told me Tonia had a twin."

The lady laughed, displaying the same dimples as her daughter. "Thank you, Colin. Coming it a little strong, perhaps, but I am pleased for the compliment, nonetheless."

The men smiled at each other amiably, and Mr. Radcliffe said, "Welcome to the family, my boy."

14

"Thank you, sir," Colin replied.

The girls linked arms with their mother and pulled her into the house with them. "Our trunks are on the way, Mama," Julia said. "Wait until you see the lovely things we brought for all of us."

"Yes," Tonia seconded. "Colin was so shocked by the mound of our luggage that he almost cried off."

"And well he might, if Julia were the prodigal you are, Antonia," her mother admonished.

"There is nothing for it," Tonia decided with a doleful face. "I shall have to marry a wealthy duke," a statement that made her sister break into laughter.

When the joke was explained to the older lady, she just shook her head. "Tonia, Tonia, you are positively incorrigible. I hope you will behave with discretion when you go to the castle, so that you do not embarrass Julia."

"Oh dear! *Now* you have quashed me," Tonia said. "I shall try to remember that admonition if I get into one of my starts."

Her mother looked at her sceptically and turned to her other daughter. "Julia, if you heed my advice, you will not take Antonia with you. She is obviously already in one of her starts."

Julia laughed and hugged her mother. "Mama, do not worry. You know that even when Tonia gets herself into a hobble, she always manages to worm out of it without the least mortification."

"Perhaps, but someday she will meet her nemesis," Mrs. Radcliffe said darkly.

"Maybe in the person of the duke," Tonia offered with a mischievous grin.

"Oh, what an impossible child," her mother said in amused exasperation. "I have spoken my piece. I can do no more. Come, let us join the gentlemen. I am anxious to become acquainted with my future son-in-law."

Colin had already come down, and the two men rose when the women entered the library. "I have been telling Mr. Radcliffe that I would be interested to hear of his latest researches and that I have been well primed," the young man said.

"Yes, Papa," Julia confirmed with a smile. "You will find Colin a good listener. He has shown the greatest tolerance for Tonia's and my expositions on any number of historical subjects."

"Good Lord! Do you mean to say that you two are in the habit of mouthing trivia?!" her father exclaimed with an expression of dismay. "You must be rated the greatest bores in Town."

"Papa!" Tonia protested in mock reproach. "How can you say so? Besides, we only mention some historical sidelight if it is pertinent to the conversation."

Mr. Radcliffe looked at Colin with respect. "I congratulate you for your forbearance, my boy. I fear it is my fault for having schooled them excessively."

"I consider it fortunate that you have, sir. Their intelligent conversations add to their charm. You were about to tell me what new project you are working on," he prompted.

"Well, I have two at the moment," Mr. Radcliffe replied. "I am writing a biography of the first Duke and Duchess of Marlborough. At the same time I am accumulating notes for a future work on the Napoleonic Wars. It is always difficult to write a definitive history on contemporary subjects, because there is so much that comes to light in subsequent decades. But I have been interviewing many veterans while events are fresh in their minds so that I will have some incidents well documented."

"Perhaps I can help you there, sir. I have been five years with the Army."

"What branch?" the historian asked eagerly.

"I was one of General Sir Thomas Picton's aides with the 3rd division in the Peninsula and then with the 5th at Waterloo."

"I hope you will not regret your rash offer, Colin. Now I have you in my hands, I cannot possibly let you go," Mr. Radcliffe warned. "I hope Julia will spare you to me an hour or two a day."

"Of course, Papa. But you know we do mean to leave for Nottinghamshire in two weeks," his daughter reminded him.

"Yes, well, it will not be enough time, though we can resume later."

"After I am acquainted with what exactly you are interested in,

Mr. Radcliffe, I will make notes when something comes to mind," Colin promised. "And I think you would be even better served if you would spend some time at the castle so that you might speak to my brother. He served Wellington these last several years and was employed in preparing and sometimes delivering dispatches. I would venture to say that he knows almost as much about the sequence of events as the Iron Duke himself. And before the Peninsular campaign he worked in the Foreign Office, somehow involved in arranging for financial aid to our allies."

"He sounds as though he would be a gold mine of information," Mr. Radcliffe remarked expectantly. "I shall count on you to arrange a meeting. Can you speak for him?"

"If you mean will he be cooperative, yes, sir, I can vouch for that," the young man answered with a grin. "When we get to the castle, I will bring it up to him. And then when it is convenient all around, we will welcome you to Glenview."

"I can see that I am to be a beneficiary in this business," Mr. Radcliffe noted.

"As may we all be," Tonia interposed with a prescient air.

"Antonia," her mother said reprovingly, "you will oblige me by refraining from engaging in these flights of whimsey. It is not becoming."

Tonia laughed at this mild reprimand. "All right, Mama—I have had my fun. Now I will go upstairs to help Janie unpack. Tomorrow when Papa and Colin are having their conference, you and Julia and I will go through our treasure trove."

That evening Mr. and Mrs. Radcliffe were pleasantly reassured as they became acquainted with their daughter's fiancé. Their own son, Marcus, in age between the two girls, had been killed five years before at the Battle of Barrosa in Spain. It had been a great blow to all of them, for he had been a dearly loved son and brother, and had shown great promise as a scholar. So Colin's advent on the scene raised expectations, especially as he showed himself to be in harmony with each of them, having a naturally sensitive disposition and finding it easy to establish

17

common ground with those he respected and loved, just as Julia did herself—a happy circumstance that augered auspiciously for their future happiness.

Before they retired, it was decided that the girls would spend the morning with their mother, so the two men were given leave to begin their studies. When they all met for lunch they would make further plans according to their inclinations.

Julia and Tonia spent the early hours organizing their belongings, and it was not until ten o'clock that they shepherded their mother to the extra bedroom where the maids had laid out the things they had brought for her approval.

Mrs. Radcliffe was only the least bit dismayed by the lavish display. She loved beautiful clothes as well as Tonia did, and she always looked forward to her daughters' return from one of their shopping sprees.

"Mama," Tonia said, "I hope you do not mind being just a trifle unfashionable. The new gowns are being shown above the ankle. But I ordered ours to fall two inches longer. Being short, as we both are, the new style would not flatter us."

"I'm sure you are right, Antonia. But do you not think you rather overdid it?" her mother asked dubiously as she eyed the stack of gowns waiting for her to try on.

"Perhaps," her daughter conceded. "But there were so many lovely things this year I could not resist. Come, let's see how they look."

Willingly Mrs. Radcliffe began to try on the gowns and the matching accessories and shoes, pronouncing herself very well pleased with all but one, which she felt was too youthful looking. "Thank you, darlings. You cannot know how gratifying it is to me not to have to shop. I find it so tedious. You must give me an accounting, and I will settle with you."

Once all this enrobing and disrobing had finished, the ladies went to the library to announce that they were ready for lunch. The gentlemen did not display any sign that they had been impatient for company, almost seeming surprised that they had been at it so long. In fact they showed a definite reluctance to put aside their project, which obviously had produced good results, if the stacks of papers told any story.

"Anne," Matthew Radcliffe said to his wife, "this boy is a wellspring of information. His memory astonishes me. And he participated in some of the most important battles of the war. But now, Colin, I had better release you, else Julia might not be so amiable about letting me claim your services next time. I will stay here to work today if you will excuse me. Go and enjoy your afternoon." And he began to order his notes.

The others left him to his work and proceeded to the dining room as the lady of the house explained, "My husband rarely eats luncheon, Colin, so you must excuse him. Later I will take him some fruit and cheese."

"He is a very impressive scholar and a canny interrogator," Colin commented admiringly. "His probings made me remember things I didn't know I knew. I am going to enjoy my sessions with him."

"Julia," Tonia teased, "I don't know if this is so much going to be a case of you gaining a husband or of Father gaining a son."

"One goes with the other, Tonia," Julia responded with a loving smile at her betrothed. "I am happy that they are so compatible. What would you like to do this afternoon, Colin?" she asked. "The property is not extensive, but Tonia and I have planted a woodland garden that is pleasant to walk through. Or we could ride if you wish though it may be warm for that now. And…"

"No, do not confuse me, darling," Colin said with a laugh. "Already I have decided. I choose a leisurely walk in your garden."

"All right," Julia agreed. "I will change shoes. Come with us, Tonia."

"Only as far as the gnarled oak," her sister replied. "I will take my paints, for I have been looking forward to working again, and that tree has been tempting me for ages."

19

"Are you a serious painter, Tonia?" Colin asked with interest.

"Well, yes," she told him. "While we are here, I will show you some of my canvases."

"She is really a very good artist, Colin," Julia boasted. "Even Mr. Constable has commented favourably on her work."

"I am impressed, Tonia. You must bring your tools to the castle. Glenview is a beautiful property, and the park has any number of spectacular views."

"Yes, I had planned to do so. I have read a description of the estate and have been anticipating the opportunity to explore the grounds. It will be interesting to compare Humphrey Repton's landscaping with that of Capability Brown at Blenheim Palace. I imagine there is much similarity, since both are reputed to employ a particular design to promote a natural effect. Last year when Papa was researching for his Marlborough biography, we all accompanied him to Oxford and made daily trips to the ducal seat so he might examine the archives there. I was able to make several sketches and completed one rather nice painting of the lake and Vanbrugh's causeway."

After they had conversed a while longer, Mrs. Radcliffe admitted herself very much taken with her daughter's fiancé. "It will be lovely to have another man in the family," she said as she smiled at Colin. "My husband dotes on the girls, of course. But he does get involved in his work and cannot be persuaded to remove himself to the fashionable haunts."

"Well, Mama, do not put all the blame on Papa," Tonia chided goodhumouredly. "You are not much for being a social butterfly yourself. You have been quite content to let Aunt Margot chaperon us. But I am not finding fault," the girl assured, noting her mother's sheepish look. "There was no reason you should be obliged to do something against your inclination. Julia and I would not have felt at all comfortable if you had forced yourself to do so just for our sakes. And as you see, at least one of us has managed very well. I expect *I* am a hopeless case—though you must not suppose it is from a want of options"—a candid assertion that in someone of a less light-mannered personality would have smacked of arrogance.

Mrs. Radcliffe decided to ignore this last provocation, though she privately resolved to go more deeply into the matter when she and Tonia were alone. She would rather learn first hand what havoc her daughter had wrought this year than hear about it in missives from friends who delighted in reporting all the little excitements that enlivened the Season.

Julia and Tonia excused themselves to put on walking shoes, and Tonia gathered her supplies—a folding stool and a canvas—from the room that had been fitted out as a studio. Julia helped her carry some of it until they descended to the hall, when Colin relieved both of them of most of their burden.

They walked across a well-manicured lawn, kept so by the sheep that roamed near the house, and entered an inviting, wooded area, following a path that wound through the trees. Presently Tonia stopped and began to set up her materials.

"This looks promising," she decided. "I shall have to mark the exact spot and return each day at this time so that the shadows will be the same. Today I will just sketch the outlines and tomorrow I'll begin painting."

The other two left her to her work and wandered on, hand in hand, perfectly happy with their privacy. Julia pointed out some of the wild flowers—violets, primroses, bluebells, yellow pimpernel, ferns, foxgloves—the remains of the crocuses and daffodils that had bloomed earlier—and they sampled the raspberries now ready for picking.

"You and Tonia may have planted the flowers, my love, but I will not allow that you contrived this little path," Colin said.

"Oh, Colin, of course not," Julia replied with a laugh. "There is a tenant who maintains it. The property is not large but there are a few acres at the west border that are farmed by Mr. Jensen and his two older sons. Papa has an agreement with him that he need only supply the household with produce and do some odd jobs outside to have the use and profits of the land he farms."

"That is a very generous arrangement," Colin remarked in surprise.

"Perhaps. But Papa feels he would rather have the land work for somebody else if he is not going to use it. And it provides a very good living for a really hard working, estimable family."

It occurred to Colin that the members of Julia's family were singularly unconcerned about money. He supposed Mr. Radcliffe had a competence outside of the remuneration he received for his books, and he knew the girls both had inherited a handsome sum. But they must be even better fixed than he had supposed. His conference with Julia's father might be a little ticklish. He himself had no fortune of his own—only a generous allowance granted by the duke—though Colin knew that Derek meant to set him up, now that they both had come home from the wars and were prepared to settle down. Still, he had nothing specific to offer at the moment.

Julia noticed his thoughtful expression, and she enquired, "What are you thinking about, Colin, that you look so serious?"

He gave her a wry grin. "I am just come to realize that while I have prospects, I am not now in a position to give an accounting to your father," he admitted. "He will have every right to show me the door."

"Colin, what are you saying!" Julia exclaimed in dismay. "After meeting him, can you actually conceive such an incivility? You are my choice, and he likes you. What else is there?"

"There are other considerations, darling," he said as he pulled her to him, "but we need not discuss them now." He kissed her hungrily and then pushed her away, saying gruffly to disguise his emotions, "Come. Let us go back to see how the artist is doing."

Tonia had nearly finished her sketch, and after a few moments began to pack her equipment. Colin picked up the stool and paint box, and they returned to the house to have a refreshing drink before going to dress for dinner.

After a leisurely meal Colin requested a private audience with his host, who had been primed earlier by his younger daughter. "Now, my boy," Mr. Radcliffe said when they had settled themselves comfortably in the library with glasses of brandy, "I do not think this is at all necessary. Julia is of age and her own mistress. But if you insist, we will air the matter. Her dowry, of course, will be her inheritance from her aunt, which brings her five thousand a year."

"That is a substantial sum," Colin noted with a rueful expression. "It makes it even more difficult for me to tell you that I am little better than a charity case. My brother controls all the family finances and has set up a generous allowance for me. I have never had cause to complain. However, this afternoon it suddenly came to me that I am in fact, to all extent and purposes, completely penniless."

"Do you have any reason to suppose that the duke will not make a settlement on you?"

"Lord no! It's only that we have been serving in the military these last several years, and the matter was not taken up. I know he means to turn over some of the property to me and no doubt already has the matter in hand."

"Oh, that is too bad," Mr. Radcliffe said with a twinkle in his eye. "I was about to offer you employment."

Colin grinned. "I shall keep that in mind if I ever find myself in dire straits, sir. I am sure I would find the work extremely gratifying."

Mr. Radcliffe leaned over to clasp his shoulder and said sincerely, "Do not concern yourself, Colin. I am very happy for you and Julia. I ask nothing more than that you love her well and treat her honourably."

"That I can promise you, sir," Colin responded fervently. "I consider myself the most fortunate of men."

When they rejoined the ladies, Julia took her fiancé by the hand and drew him outside. They walked with arms around each other in the fading twilight while Colin described his conference with her father.

"So it is all happily settled," Julia remarked with satisfaction. "At least on my end."

"You are not to worry about my family, darling," Colin said

firmly. "I will not permit any interference. I do not promise you they will be so readily agreeable as your family has been, but you may trust me to carry the day."

"I do trust you, Colin. And I will not play the milk-and-water miss in this matter, I can tell you," Julia said staunchly.

"And perhaps we are being unnecessarily dubious," Colin added. "There might not be any trouble at all."

"You are quite right, my love," said Julia. "So I shall believe until we face the test. We'll not let doubts cast a shadow on our happy hours here."

═══3═══

THE NEXT FEW days passed pleasantly. Colin was drawn more and more closely into the family. Having led a somewhat unstable existence the past few years as the battlegrounds advanced through the Peninsula into France, he found the security and intimacy of this new adventure into domesticity uncommonly alluring.

The young people usually rode out before breakfast, and then Colin spent an hour or two with Mr. Radcliffe, sessions both men found extremely stimulating. After lunch Tonia returned to her retreat to work on her painting, and Julia and Colin sought their own amusements in the vicinity.

During one of their excursions, Mrs. Radcliffe finally claimed her older daughter's company to learn of the major *on dit* of this year's Season. "I am particularly anxious to know if we are to receive any complaints from outraged mamas who might imagine their sons had been treated cavalierly."

"Mama! Surely you do not take such imputations seriously," Tonia protested with an aggrieved expression. "You know that some women are so impressed with their offspring that they cannot conceive that others might not share their opinion. Unfortunately some gentlemen think very highly of themselves, also, and imagine they have only to throw their handkerchiefs for the ladies they favour to drop to their knees to pick them up. It is *quite* ridiculous!" she said indignantly.

Mrs. Radcliffe closed her eyes and resigned herself to hearing the worst at once. "How many this time, Tonia?"

"Only three," a quavering voice answered.

"Who were they? Must we expect repercussions?"

"Well, perhaps you may hear of *one* unfortunate *contretemps.* The others took it better."

"Who did not?" Mrs. Radcliffe pressed.

"Young Lord Smithson. I suppose I was a little careless. But I keep thinking my advanced age would be something of a deterrent, though it appears I have misjudged that. You see, Lord Edmund is a special friend of Colin's—a very likeable, handsome young man but definitely *young* in comparison. It was very pleasant to go about as a foursome. I thought I behaved in a rather motherly—or at least sisterly—way towards him. However, he became hopelessly enamoured. I had to dash his hopes abruptly. Still he persisted, making a cake of himself, until Colin took a hand in it and told him to stop annoying me. He left town in a huff, and his mother and sister cut me for the rest of the Season."

"Oh dear! I *could* wish, Tonia, that you would accept an offer so you do not continue to create these scandals. I must say that you have shown yourself too particular. There have been several exceptional gentlemen you could have married."

"But none I wanted to, Mama. Surely you would not wish me to marry just to take myself out of circulation? I would rather become a recluse."

"Tonia, don't be absurd. You know I do not mean to push you. It's just that I think you are being much too nice. What of the Earl of Atlee?"

"He wasn't in Town this year—which *is* rather strange," Tonia mused, having often wondered about that these past few months. "But while I do like him better than any other, Mama, you must not think I mean to accept him eventually, for I do not. He has far too little spirit and I am afraid I should be bored beyond endurance."

"All right, my love. I'm sure you know best. I just wanted to know what tales would come to our ears. You do have a penchant for creating a stir. Now, apart from your flirtations, what else do you have to report?"

Tonia wrinkled her nose at this casual accusation and told her mother that she was sure her little peccadilloes would go unremarked, as society was all agog over the departure of two of its most flamboyant members. Lord Byron and "Beau" Brummell

26

had fled to the Continent to escape their financial and personal difficulties. She then spoke of the intention of Lady Margot and Lady Samantha to go to the United States in the fall.

"Those two ever have some mad escapade up their sleeves," Mrs. Radcliffe said with a laugh. "One would think they were in the first bloom of youth—or in their dotage."

"Lots of people journey to America, Mama," Tonia said in defense of the two ladies.

"Perhaps they do at that," her mother conceded. "Though I doubt there are many middle-aged females out for a lark."

"No, truly, they want to see their sons and grandchildren," Tonia iterated and then changed the subject, knowing that her mother's conservative outlook precluded any instinctive sympathy with her sister-in-law's more venturesome nature.

"Isn't it fine that Julia and Colin found each other?" she asked her mother. "I wish you could have been there to see it develop. It was the loveliest thing. Colin is absolutely the most wonderful gentleman. I have never met anyone who can compare to him. I am quite jealous of Julia."

"Tonia," her mother asked fearfully, "surely you are not in love with him also?"

Tonia laughed delightedly and reassured her mother, "No, Mama, not like that. I dearly love him, but as I did Mark. No more than that, I promise you. It's just that I am so pleased with the match and know him for a superior gentleman, as Julia has told you. They will be very happy once he reconciles his family."

"He is expecting opposition?" Mrs. Radcliffe asked uneasily, always having had an aversion to discord.

"From his mother, at least. But you are not to worry about it. I have every confidence in him. He has a great deal of character and resolve."

"It's only to be expected, I suppose," the older lady allowed unhappily. "I am glad you are going along to offer Julia support."

Two pleasant weeks passed quickly. In the third week of June, as planned, a venturesome threesome took leave of the senior Radcliffes, heading for the road that led to the duke's hunting box near Oakham in Leicestershire, where they would stop overnight.

In the late afternoon they turned off the main road to follow a narrow drive, soon coming upon an unexpectedly large edifice which prompted Tonia to ask skeptically, "*This* is a hunting box?"

"So we have come to call it," Colin replied. "Actually it is one of our smaller properties. But since it is so near the castle, we do not use it as a residence."

"It looks charming," Julia said. "I am glad we are staying here instead of at some noisy inn."

Both carriages pulled to a stop, and a weary group gathered in the courtyard. The coachman and outriders were directed to the stables while the others made for the house. A moment after Colin sounded the knocker, an elderly servant opened the door and exclaimed with pleasure, "Lord Colin! I was wonderin' if you would be comin' through. The duke stopped by a few days ago with Lord Atlee and said you would be a-meetin' him at the castle."

"And so I am, Potkin. But tonight we mean to rest here. You may wish me happy, you know," Colin said with a broad smile, taking Julia's hand and bringing her forward. "This is Miss Julia Radcliffe, my promised bride, and her sister Miss Antonia Radcliffe."

The old man's eyes lit up with interest. He bowed and said, "Welcome to Sayer's Lodge, Miss Julia and Miss Radcliffe, My wife and I will be delighted to serve you. And I *am* wishin' you happy, Mr. Colin. If you will excuse me, I will tell the missus. She will be pleased to see you."

A moment later he returned, following a spritely white-haired little woman who came to welcome the travellers. She took special notice of the two girls as she congratulated Colin. "It is time you boys were settling down now that the wars are over. Come, my ladies, I will show you to your rooms. I'll give them the master suite, Mr. Colin. You and your attendant can have the smaller apartment," she said as she led the way to the bedrooms.

28

When she had situated the girls in a large room with an oversized bed and opened a connecting door to a smaller room for their maid, she hurried off to prepare a special dinner to celebrate their arrival.

Tonia and Julia rested for an hour and then began to dress for dinner, choosing formal gowns to show their appreciation of Mrs. Potkin's desire to honour Julia and Colin's betrothal. Colin, too, had dressed for the occasion, so it was an elegant threesome that sat down to a delicious dinner of several courses, to which they did credit. They dined leisurely and later sat before a fire that had been built to ward off the chill of the evening.

"We need not rise too early tomorrow," Colin informed the girls when they were making ready to retire. "As the castle is only a little over thirty miles away, it will be an easy trip."

4

TONIA WAKENED a little early but lay quietly so as not to disturb Julia. She reflected on the strange coincidence of the obviously close connection between the Duke of Sayer and the Earl of Atlee. She wondered if the friendship were of longstanding. There must be at least four years difference between the two men—the earl was a widower with a sixteen-year-old daughter, and she knew that he had been of age when he first married. Tonia had met him five years ago at the house party of a mutual friend. From the beginning he had attached himself to her and had proposed within a month. She liked him very well but, as she told her mother, not enough to marry him. He had never really accepted her refusal, though he had continued his courtship in such an inoffensive and gentle fashion that Tonia had not felt compelled to deny herself the pleasure of his very agreeable companionship. In fact she had missed his presence this Season. Perhaps he had finally resigned himself and had joined his friend in other pastimes. With a faint pang of regret she speculated that even the most faithful suitor could not be expected to wait in the wings indefinitely.

Julia stirred and murmured, "Tonia?"

"Yes, love, I'm awake, though I am already become weary from having been thinking so hard."

"What about?" Julia asked as she sat up and stretched.

"About what a small world it is—the fact that Atlee seems to be a good friend of the duke."

"Yes, I thought about that, too. Do you suppose he will be at Glenview?"

"I don't know. He could just be on his way to Lincolnshire."

"Well, I hope he does not join us. It would be very uncomfortable for you to have him at such close quarters. And it certainly would be difficult for him, as he does love you truly," Julia said sympathetically.

"Yes, it is one thing to be friendly with him in company. But in an intimate group, it would be a bit ticklish," Tonia reflected.

After passing through Melton Mowbray, which was the center of the famous hunting country, the carriages continued on to Nottingham, where they crossed the River Trent. "We have only a few miles now," Colin informed his companions. "The estate borders the river, but the main entrance is at the opposite end."

Presently they arrived at the gate, and the coachman sounded his horn, bringing the gatekeeper at a run. As he recognized Colin's driver, the guard quickly cleared the way. Both carriages then proceeded spankingly through rows of soaring trees that formed a lovely filigreed canopy. Almost a mile farther along they finally came upon the castle which sat on a hill overlooking the river.

"I am already impressed, Colin," Tonia remarked. "The setting is beautiful. And I am happy to see that it is a *real* castle!"

"What do you mean by that, Tonia?" Colin asked.

"One with a round tower and castellated walls. Some stately houses are called castles but just look like country houses. Is it all in repair?"

"Well, none of it is in danger of collapsing, though we have closed off a good part of it. It's very large. There are one hundred twenty rooms in all, and the older section just isn't conducive to comfortable living. But we do maintain the watchtower. There is something soul-stirring about climbing to the top to survey the countryside."

"Yes, I imagine there is, especially when you know that your ancestors have been doing so for generations," Tonia observed.

Two young stable hands came to hold the horses as the carriages drew up in the courtyard.

Colin escorted his guests to the massive oak door and thumped the heavy knocker. Immediately the door glided open soundlessly, to the girls' surprise; having been influenced by the

Gothic romances they had read, they had expected a portentous creaking. A footman stood back, and an elegant butler came forward to relieve Colin of his hat, which he immediately handed to his underling. "Welcome home, Lord Colin."

"Thank you, Nestor. We were expected, I trust?"

"Yes, my lord. We received your message a week ago, and all is in readiness."

"Good. Our guests are Miss Julia and her sister Miss Radcliffe. Is my aunt about?"

"I believe the mistress has just risen from her afternoon nap, Lord Colin. We did not expect you until after five."

"Well, then, will you have Mrs. Hopkins show the ladies to their rooms and then direct the porters to dispose of the baggage?"

"Yes, my lord. If the ladies will follow me, I will show them to their rooms myself and will send Mrs. Hopkins to them directly."

Looking at each other in amusement, the girls scurried to follow the obviously consequential majordomo as he led them up the stairs to the second floor, down a long hall lined with portraits and statuary to a pair of rooms joined by a connecting door. Both rooms had a view of the river, and Julia exclaimed delightedly, "Oh, this is perfect. I am sure we will be very comfortable here."

With a not-quite-deferential bow, the butler left them to settle in, and a few minutes later they were joined by a large, jolly-faced woman, dressed in the traditional black bombazine, who stood in marked contrast to the impassive, staid Nestor. She welcomed them effusively, declaring, "Well, you are both beauties. But which of you is Miss Julia?"

"I am, Mrs. Hopkins"—an admission that invited a fervent embrace from the good woman.

"I can tell you that the household has been all that excited to meet you, my dears, ever since we received Lord Colin's letter."

"Even Nestor?" Tonia asked mischievously.

"Now don't you be letting that grand gentleman put you out of countenance, Miss. He's all show—a taskmaster, maybe, but not the least bearish underneath. Is there anything I can do for you?"

"Perhaps you would order baths for us, Mrs. Hopkins," Julia said diffidently.

"The water is being heated now. The girls will be bringing it in a few minutes. It is carried some distance, so you had best be ready to use it immediately, while it is still warm."

"And how soon shall we come downstairs?" Tonia asked.

"Why, as soon as you are ready, Miss Radcliffe. Lady Alvinia will be very upset that she was not prepared to come down to greet you when you arrived. I am sure she will be waiting for you in the main drawing room. It's on the first floor, just at the head of the stairs."

"We'll hurry, then," Julia said as she turned to have Tonia unbutton her gown. With an approving smile, the housekeeper tactfully left them to their ministrations.

"Well, Julia," Tonia said, when they had bathed and dressed in new gowns, "let us go to meet Lady Alvinia. Perhaps we can enlist a sponsor before our time of trial."

"Tonia, what an absolute card you are," Julia said with a laugh. "I don't know how you can pretend you are the least bit daunted by our prospects when you haven't a reverent bone in your body."

When they entered the drawing room, Colin came to take Julia by the hand and led her to a grey-haired lady sitting in a straight-backed chair next to a tea table. "Aunt Alvinia, I am very pleased to introduce you to my fiancée, Miss Julia Radcliffe, and her sister, Miss Antonia Radcliffe."

Leaning on a cane, Lady Alvinia rose slowly and greeted them with a friendly smile. "I am happy to meet you both. I have been anticipating your visit since Colin wrote to tell me his very welcome news. I am relieved he does not mean to follow in the footsteps of the head of this family."

The girls laughed, both liking this fragile-looking maiden aunt immediately. Julia said sweetly, "Thank you, Lady Alvinia. We, too, have been looking forward to coming here to meet Colin's family."

"Well, perhaps we will have a few days to become well acquainted before the others arrive," Colin's aunt commented hopefully. "It is my intention to leave shortly thereafter to visit other relations."

"Aunt Alvinia, surely you and my mother have patched up your differences by now," Colin chided, understanding what was left unsaid by this communication.

"My dear, it is not that we are at odds, and certainly not for that old reason, but you know Lady Merrill has a very proprietary air when she is in residence. It is just not comfortable for the two of us to be here at the same time, for there are factions among the servants. It will be a good opportunity for me to make a tour. Now, we must not give the girls the impression that they have come upon a tinder box, for that is not really the case. It only needs a little restraint to keep the peace."

Try as she might, Tonia could not help but laugh. "Lady Alvinia, I have a feeling that might be something of an understatement, if you are so ready to take wing. The implication is most intriguing, and I daresay some sparks are going to fly."

"Very likely, Antonia," the lady replied dryly as she limped back to sit down. "Do make yourselves comfortable, and we will have some tea. Draw up some chairs, Colin. Sit here by me, Miss Julia."

"Just Julia, Lady Alvinia."

"Yes," Tonia agreed. "for we shall definitely have to speed our progression to intimacy if you mean to desert us so soon."

Lady Alvinia looked at her sharply and asked bluntly, "How old are you, Antonia?"

"Twenty-nine."

"Well, that does explain your provocative self-confidence, though it is hard to credit you are that old. How is it you have never married?"

"I have never been tempted—might I ask the same of you?"

"I have always been afflicted," Lady Alvinia stated simply.

"Afflicted? Is that how you characterize your limp?"

"So I was taught to do early in life," the old lady said with a wry face.

"Why, how perfectly absurd!" Julia cried indignantly.

Lady Alvinia's countenance lightened. "Yes, I concluded that myself eventually," she admitted with a little smile. "However, by then I had come to be jealous of my independence, and I was not disposed to change my lot. But now let us put aside such ancient matters and speak of the future. Has Derek said what he plans to do for you now that you are to be married, Colin?"

"He doesn't know yet that I am. I haven't had contact with him since before I went to London. When do you expect him home?"

"Within the week, if he follows the schedule he set down in his last letter. And when do you expect your mother?" Lady Alvinia asked.

"Fairly soon. Immediately she gets word, I imagine," Colin replied with a grin.

Lady Alvinia looked at both girls searchingly and observed from their expressions of amusement that they were aware of a possible hurdle and did not seem dismayed by the prospect. So she refrained from making any further allusions in that vein and turned the conversation instead to learning more about these two lovely ladies who were to become a part of her intimate circle. She found it very easy to like both girls and readily understood why Colin had singled out Julia, whom she recognized as a sensible, lovely young woman who would make an exceptional wife. But she had to admit to a partiality for Antonia, whose irrepressible sense of humour and pithy remarks she found diverting. She might stay about, after all, she mused, having an interesting presentiment that the summer at Glenview would prove to be more than usually entertaining.

After she had retired to her chamber, Colin revealed the history of the disaffection between his mother and his aunt. "Aunt Alvinia was especially cherished by my father so there was some competition involved. But more than that, she was Derek's mother's best friend, and she rather resented it when Father remarried after Lady Anne's death, even though he waited almost six years. It didn't make it any more palatable that he was thirty-eight and my mother seventeen.

"I suspect that Aunt Alvinia's skepticism had some basis at first.

The marriage had been arranged by my father and Mother's father, and I don't doubt some money changed hands. My grandfather had long had a reputation for being something of a wastrel. But even so, the connexion proved to be reasonably happy. My mother is a very impressionable woman, and she forms sincere attachments to people who are important in her life and who show her affection."

"It does create problems when there are complicated family relationships," Tonia remarked understandingly. "But surely they have reached an accommodation by now."

"Yes, though as a matter of habit they do a little backbiting, which the rest of us ignore. And Aunt Alvinia usually decamps for a while," Colin said with a wry smile.

"Does your aunt live here permanently?" Julia inquired.

"Yes. She has always lived at Glenview. For a while, until my mother came, she was mistress here and now is again, of course, at Derek's request. However, her actual duties are minimal, mainly because Nestor and Mrs. Hopkins are very solicitous of her and contrive to keep the household operating efficiently so there will not be too much on her shoulders. She is not really very strong, you see, and tires easily. Now you both must be burnt to a socket yourselves," Colin noted. "It has been a long day, so I shall send you to bed. Sleep as long as you like tomorrow. Then later we will ride around the estate."

In the morning Tonia wakened early, as usual, and called Janie to help her wash her hair. She stepped out on the narrow balcony to let it dry and studied the landscape before her. On this, the river side, the ground had been terraced away from the castle to moderate the slope of the hill. Yet the mounds were staggered and irregular, and the path that led to the river curved to follow the naturally contrived contour. Repton reportedly had a dislike of straight lines, and even his avenues and drives never were planned in such a manner. In the early days of the castle, the approach was no doubt kept free of tall growth so that the fortress could be more easily defended. But now there was extensive planting, and the combination of stretches of lawn and non-uniform clumps of trees—Lebanon cedars, oaks, beeches, hollies, thorns and sycamores—gave the massive structure a parklike setting that pleased Tonia's artistic eye. Looking straight down, she examined the walled terrace, adjacent to the castle. It was obviously maintained by a meticulous gardener, and there was a profusion of roses in their second bloom of the season. What a lovely place, Tonia thought. She could hardly wait to begin exploring, both inside and out. Turning as Julia entered, she invited her to share the view.

"Rather spectacular, isn't it?" she asked dreamily.

"And it's a beautiful day, too," Julia replied cheerfully. "Come on. Pin up your hair, and we will go down to look for Colin."

A few minutes later they peered into the morning room to find a neatly uniformed young maid who seemed to have been waiting for them. She curtsied and then scurried from the room. Almost immediately the estimable butler appeared to inform them that Lord Colin had gone out to the stables and had asked to be called when the ladies had finished breakfast. "I will send word to the kitchen that you have come down."

"Thank you, Nestor. Will Lady Alvinia be joining us?" Tonia asked.

"No, Miss Radcliffe. The mistress always takes the morning meal in her chambers while she confers with Mrs. Hopkins."

"I see. Well then, please tell the cook that we would just like some fruit and coffee—and perhaps a muffin."

"Very well, Miss Radcliffe."

Just as they were finishing this light meal, Colin came in to see if they were ready for an excursion. Finding both ladies eager to explore, he had the horses brought around at once and helped them to mount. They followed a path leading to the river, riding leisurely, so as to enjoy the varied views, and occasionally stopping to examine some unusual horticultural specimen or to admire a particularly pleasing vista. At one point Colin directed their attention to a barely perceptible outline of a domed temple. It had been built in the early part of the previous century by an ancestor who had just returned from a Grand Tour, during which he had developed an admiration for the classical Greek and Roman buildings. "We will go that way later," he said.

When they reached the river, they turned back to look up at the castle, which appeared to be sitting on the treetops.

"Well, Colin, impressed is not the word for it," Tonia said feelingly. "I am enraptured. Why, I have already seen so much I would like to paint, I won't know where to start."

"You have the whole summer, Tonia. And, for that matter, a lifetime. You could make Glenview your special subject and record it for posterity."

"What a lofty-sounding ambition, Colin. I can see that I will certainly have to mind my steps with the duke," Tonia said, prompting her companions to laugh.

They walked their horses for a while along the river and then mounted again to head in the direction of the little temple. It stood on the edge of a small lake that was completely surrounded by a charming landscape heavy with shrubbery, evergreens and stately trees. Other trees, young in comparison, had no doubt been planted by Repton when he laid out the grounds twenty years before. In relief there were patches of lawn and winding paths. Tethering their horses, they followed one of these latter that led to the temple.

"It is not very large," Colin remarked as they came upon it, "as you see."

"It would be incongruous if it were," Tonia judged, "since the lake is small. The proportions are compatible now. Which came first, Colin?"

"The lake. It rises from a spring and is the source of the water pumped into the house. The mechanism is on the other side, hidden by that large clump of shrubbery. Come. Let us walk around the shore." The walk proved to be longer than it had appeared; the size of the lake, snug in its artfully sculptured setting, was deceptive. When they returned to their horses, Colin led the way back to the castle. All three retired to their rooms to refresh themselves and change from their riding habits. In the drawing room, they found Lady Alvinia waiting for them with lemonade and little tea cakes.

"Do come eat something," she said in welcome. "I know you did not eat much this morning and are likely starved."

"Lady Alvinia, you are a trump," Tonia declared gratefully. "We were gone quite a long time, and my stomach, if you will excuse such an unmaidenly expression, has been complaining."

"And how did you enjoy your day?" Lady Alvinia asked.

"Oh, it was lovely. And Tonia is going to paint any number of scenes," Julia said enthusiastically.

"For posterity," Colin added with a grin.

"I will be very much interested to see your work, Antonia," Lady Alvinia told her.

"Well, I hope you also will show us the tapestries that Colin tells us you have made, and are working on, to record the history of the Neville family," Tonia said.

"I will be happy to, my dear. It has been my life work—and is also meant for posterity."

The next day Tonia was determined to get an early start on her first painting. But just when she was about to ask Colin and Julia to help her haul her materials to the site she had chosen, they heard the sound of horses coming up the drive. In a moment two riders, a lady and an attendant, appeared and pulled to a halt in front of the castle.

Colin moved to help a dark-haired, buxom young woman dismount. "Hello, Alicia," he greeted her. "Have you come to meet my guests?"

The lady laughed. "Yes, I have. There is a servant grapevine, as you know, and I naturally am curious."

Colin grinned and escorted her to where the girls were standing, saying, "Julia, darling, and Tonia, may I introduce Baroness Alicia Ealand, our neighbour?—Miss Julia and Miss Antonia Radcliffe, Alicia."

The ladies looked at each other with interest. Tonia, from years of experience in observing the fashionable temptresses of society, immediately identified the Baroness as a candidate for membership in that sisterhood. She was certainly a luscious-looking woman. Tonia wondered if her naturally bold manner and her flamboyant appearance were a fair indication of her true personality.

"Colin, how dare you bring two such beauties into our midst?"

Lady Alicia chided goodhumouredly. If the lady did feel a certain inner resentment, her faint disaffection was of no great magnitude. She had heard that Julia was safely betrothed to Colin, and, peculiarly, it did not once occur to the baroness that Tonia posed any threat to her ambition, a miscalculation she was to marvel at in the not-too-distant future. Being well satisfied with her own spectacular Junoesque form, she was oblivious to Tonia's equally appealing, if less blatant, charms.

"I have a purpose to introduce my fiancée to the family, Alicia," Colin told her. "I suppose you also know that?"

"Of course," the baroness replied. "And I hope you will postpone whatever you had planned for the moment so that we may all become acquainted." Looking quizzingly at the artist's paraphernalia, she inquired, "Come now. What are you about?"

"Tonia paints, baroness," Julia replied. "And we were just going to help her set up her easel in the lower garden."

"That can wait, Julia," Tonia demurred, not entirely resigned, but admittedly intrigued by this visitor.

"Good," the baroness said. "Now you must tell me how all transpired and what plans you have made."

Both girls quickly formed a distinct impression that there was something suspect about this lady's intentions. Nevertheless, she seemed to be remarkably good-natured, and though there was a streak of brashness in her manner, neither Julia nor Tonia was particularly put off by it. With their usual amiability, they were inclined to accept her offered friendship at face value.

She remained to take lunch with them. Then, after paying her respects to Lady Alvinia and learning that the duke was expected in a day or two, she rode off with her groom.

"Well, now, Colin, you will please set us straight in the matter of the baroness, so we can judge just how sincere she is in her professions of friendship," Tonia said quizzically.

Both Colin and Lady Alvinia had to laugh. "Your perceptions are quick, Tonia. Obviously she has an eye out for Derek," Colin acknowledged.

"Is she recently widowed?" Julia asked innocently.

"No, the baron is very much alive," Lady Alvinia replied with a certain hint of acid in her voice, "but she does not consider that a deterrent. Since May she has been coming here at least once a week on an ostensible 'duty-call' though she never fails to ask when Derek is coming home. I'll have to say she is not the least coy about it."

Seeing that Tonia and Julia waited expectantly to hear more, Colin shook his head in amusement. "All right. I suppose you may as well hear the story," he said. "It is really not all that scandalous except for Alicia's undisguised passion. She is the daughter of Lord Jamison, whose property is a few miles from here. She developed a *tendre* for Derek when she was still in the schoolroom, more than fifteen years ago. He never gave her a second thought in that way, however. So, when he left for the wars, she resigned herself to marrying Baron Ealand, who was enough attracted by her ample charms to ignore her mercenary motive for accepting his proposal. When we were here earlier in the year, it was evident that she still had designs on Derek, despite his lack of interest. It is apparent that we are going to see a great deal of her."

"I'm afraid you're right," Lady Alvinia remarked in disapproval. "You brother always did say, in private, of course, that she had the heart of a *demimondaine*. It's a good thing the baron knows Derek would not try to cuckold him or we would have the scenario for a monumental scandal."

"Lady Alvinia, how can you possibly think of leaving us when this summer at Glenview promises to afford so much excitement?" Tonia asked with a mischievous grin.

"I have considered that myself," the older lady admitted with an answering twinkle, "and I have decided to stay to watch the fun."

= 5 =

THE NEXT TWO days passed pleasurably. All the members of the household applied themselves to their own concerns and amusements. Tonia spent a good part of her time on her canvas; Lady Alvinia worked diligently on her tapestry; and Julia and Colin walked the path of lovers, blissfully happy in each other's company, planning for their future.

Alicia paid them another visit, but did not stay long, since her prey had still not arrived. And, indeed, there was a general air of expectancy in the castle as everyone awaited the next encounter.

"Do you think the duke will approve of Colin and Julia's betrothal?" Tonia asked Lady Alvinia as they sat talking one afternoon.

"I don't see why not. He is not at all high in the instep. Not, of course, that there is any reason for him to look down his nose in this instance. And even if there were, he is not of such a lordly nature that he would not acknowledge Colin's right to direct his own life."

"I am glad to hear you say so," Tonia said in relief. "I admit to having some peculiar queasiness recently, and I cannot think why."

"Julia and Colin do not seem to share your apprehensions," Lady Alvinia said.

"No, they are so high in the clouds, I doubt they could recognize a set-back if they met one," Tonia commented with her impish smile.

The two lovers came in then, and Julia joined Tonia in persuading Lady Alvinia to show them the part of the tapestry she had already finished. With Colin's help, the elderly lady climbed two flights of stairs to the floor where the girls were accommodated. She led the way to a room on the north side where she kept the tapestry. As they entered the dark room, Colin picked up a candelabra that sat on a near table and lit the candles before going to separate the draperies. He came back to hold the light so the girls might see the intricate stitches more clearly, and Lady Alvinia began to tell them what the scene depicted.

"It is the fashion of many houses to claim descent from the Norman nobles who came with the Conqueror. But our own claim is well documented, and so I began with their arrival in England," she said as she pointed out a ship in the upper left corner. With pride and ardour she continued her story, progressing to the end of the three-foot by twelve-foot panel, which had been pieced together as each section was finished.

"But why do you not hang it where it can be enjoyed?" Tonia protested. "It is incredibly beautiful."

"Thank you, Antonia. Derek, too, has expressed just such a thought. He means to prepare a special place for it soon. We have discussed the wall in the Long Gallery."

Colin and Julia had just gone down to help Tonia carry her materials back to the house the next afternoon when they heard the sound of a carriage travelling rapidly up the drive.

"Well," Colin said, "Derek has arrived at last."

"Does he always drive at such a hell-bent pace?" Tonia asked dryly.

"Often enough," Colin confirmed with a smile. "But he's a prime whip and knows what he's about. Shall we go to welcome him?"

Julia and Tonia looked at each other significantly, and Julia suggested, "Colin, I think you should see him first, to break the news. I will wait here for a few minutes."

"Julia, don't be a little goose. There is nothing to worry about," Colin protested.

"I know, my love. But I do wish you would humour me in this. I am thinking how it would be with me were our roles reversed."

"As you wish," Colin said with an amused expression, leaning down to kiss the tip of her nose. He then hurried to meet his brother and entered the house just as the Duke of Sayer was asking his whereabouts.

"It's good to see you, Colin," an elegantly dressed gentleman said sincerely, grasping him firmly on the shoulder. "I have been looking forward to a pleasant summer together."

"Where the devil have you been?" Colin asked. "I had no idea how to catch up with you."

"I've been making a tour of all the properties," the duke informed the younger man. "Now that we are to take up our responsibilities, I decided I had best see how things were going at our various holdings."

"And what did you find?" Colin asked, trying not to be impatient, though he was ready to burst with his own news.

"Some good, some bad, but, unfortunately, except for Glen-view, none excellently."

"Anything that can be remedied?"

"Perhaps. But we will discuss that later. Now, how are things with you?"

"They are wonderful, Derek," Colin replied with a broad smile. "I am extremely happy to tell you that I am to be married—to the loveliest girl imaginable."

With a look of disbelief, the duke blurted, "You *what?*"

"Come on, old man," Colin said jocularly, "it is a rather common prospect, you know, though you have seen fit to avoid the institution."

"My God!" the duke exploded, now fully alert to his brother's exultant mood. "Are you telling me that you managed to get trapped by some designing female the moment you put yourself on the Marriage Mart?"

"No," Colin answered with deceptive calm, "I said I was going to marry a lovely girl—whom I adore with all my heart."

"If I had had any idea you could not be trusted to resist being caught for just two short months, I would have taken you with me!" his grace fumed. "We shall have to find some way of getting you out of it."

"Derek, have you run mad?" Colin expostulated. "How can you stand there like a blockhead, making those damnable insulting charges, and not comprehend what I am telling you? I am going to marry Julia. I have brought her here to meet you."

"Here? She is here?" the duke sputtered with a dazed expression.

"Yes. And I thank God I allowed her to convince me to tell you of our betrothal first. If you had spoken in such galling terms before my promised wife, I would feel obliged to call you out."

"*Now* which of us is run mad?" the duke asked caustically. "We had best both control our tempers and try to sort this out. How could you be ensnared by some chit—"

"Julia is not a 'chit'," Colin told him coldly. "She is twenty-three."

"Worse yet—practically an ape-leader," the duke noted ungallantly.

"My dear brother, how is it I never truly realised what a poor opinion of women you have?"

"There is reason for it," the duke reminded him. "And you would do well to be guided by me lest you be burned, also."

"Guided by you! Those days are past, as I thought you had realised these last several years. And I'll be damned if I'll be guided by some bad-tempered cynic who thinks, just because *he* was gullible enough to be led a merry dance by some unscrupulous jade when he was still wet behind the ears, that no one else is capable of more discernment!" Colin said recklessly, impulsively straining the bond of affection and respect that had held him so tightly to his brother.

The vehemence of this accusation gave the duke a shock and a sense of loss. He realized he was forfeiting his high standing with his brother, whom he had always regarded as the most important of his many responsibilities. The thought gave him pause for a moment. Then, with a less than thorough examination of his motives, he decided that he could not permit Colin to ruin his life—particularly as he had other plans for him. He resolved to send the girl packing—would buy her off if necessary.

"Well, you might as well tell me who she is," he said ungraciously.

With clear antagonism, Colin replied, "Her name is Julia Radcliffe."

"And what is her background?" his grace pursued.

"She is the daughter of Matthew Radcliffe, who is a renowned historian."

"Radcliffe…" the duke mused. "Yes, I have heard of him. At least she has some claim to quality."

Colin could not trust himself to speak. He eyed his brother angrily.

"No doubt she would be delighted to unite herself with this family," the duke remarked acerbicly.

"She will be delighted to unite herself with *me*," Colin retorted.

"*And* your consequence?"

"Just what *is* my consequence?" Colin asked with narrowed eyes, forcing the issue.

"Only what I choose to give you," the duke responded rashly, goaded by his brother's belligerence.

"I thought we might be coming to that," Colin said. The pain in his eyes almost persuaded the duke to abandon his resolution. "So, am I to understand that if I go against you in this, I may consider myself a penniless relative?"

"I don't want that, Colin," his brother denied firmly, trying to mitigate their hostile exchanges. "You know that I wish to share the inheritance with you."

"But on your terms?" Colin asked sharply.

"Colin, I ask you to hear me out. I have been to Atlee Hall. While there I met Robert's daughter, a lovely girl of sixteen who would make you an excellent wife. Atlee and I have settled it all between us. They are coming next week to discuss the arrangements."

Colin stared at his brother incredulously. "You and Atlee have settled it between you? If I didn't know better, I would think this was some kind of bad dream," he proclaimed in disgust. "How

46

dare you think you could choose my wife? You must be barmy! I regret that you have put yourself in such a ludicrous position, my lord duke. But when your guests arrive, I will be delighted to introduce them to my beloved Julia."

"And how will she react when she knows you have no prospects?" his brother taunted.

"I'll go to learn that now, your grace. I hope you will be able to behave with civility when I introduce her and her sister to you," Colin remarked disrespectfully, and he left a furious gentleman to his own virulent thoughts.

Still shaking with anger, Colin stomped out of the house. But as he looked up to see Julia and Tonia coming towards him, the enormity of his situation struck him. He sank helplessly onto the stone bench of the walled terrace, and as his violent resentment began to fade, a wave of sadness spread over him. He had been looking forward to introducing Julia to his brother with blithe anticipation, never once imagining that Derek would try to cut up his happiness. It was hard to credit that they had flown out at each other in that reckless tirade. Such a scene had never been played before. It seemed now that the duke saw his brother merely as a jackstraw.

Julia hurried to him and kneeled before him, taking his hands in hers. "Colin, what is it?" she asked anxiously.

"Julia, I don't know how to tell you. I can hardly believe it myself. I have just received the shock of my life. I seem never to have known Derek at all." He buried his head in Julia's hair.

The two girls looked at each other in perplexity.

"Well," Tonia remarked, "so much for the duke's benevolent eye."

Taking a deep breath, Colin rose and began to pace back and forth. "Never in my wildest imagination could I have conceived of such a blow as I have just been dealt. He actually threatens to cut me off if I marry without his consent. It's incredible."

"And he does not consent?" Julia asked softly.

"Without even having met you, darling, he has formed a prejudice. I'm afraid my brother has no great opinion of women

47

and certainly has no conception of the emotion of true love." Once again he sat down and put his head in his hands, a posture that was observed by the troubled eyes of a frustrated gentleman who shamelessly looked down on the scene.

"Where is this absurd character?" Tonia asked militantly.

"In the library," Colin replied absently.

Tonia turned toward the house, and Julia protested, "Oh, Tonia, you are not truly going to try to beard the lion in his den, are you? I beg you not to exacerbate the situation."

"Don't worry, Julia, I just mean to have a look at him," Tonia said darkly. With a determined step she marched straight to the library door, where she stopped purposefully to scrutinize the lone occupant of the room, who had remarked her appearance and returned her examination in silence.

Tonia studied his countenance, surprised by his lack of resemblance to Colin. He was not as tall, though still probably close to six feet. And he had dark brown hair with a distinguished streak of grey at his temples. His build was, well, almost slight, but definitely muscular and well-proportioned. Tonia found it difficult to cast him in the role of villain until she noticed the sardonic expression and felt his eyes raking her insolently. "Yes," she decided, "he would not like to be crossed."

The duke found this silent appraisal extremely uncomfortable, though he took some pains to disguise the fact. Determined to give her her own back, he stood his ground, returning her scrutiny. This would be the sister, he surmised. Older, he gathered—a real ape-leader, though she looked a saucy chit, except for that squirrel's nest on the top of her head. As she casually leaned against the door and looked at him as if he were some sort of creature in a circus, he found himself wanting to shake her violently, an impulse intensified when suddenly, without a word, she turned away and disappeared. Clenching his fists, the duke steeled himself to keep from going after her and punishing her for her damned cheekiness. He was not accustomed to being treated so disrespectfully. If this show of insolence was a mirror of the sister's attitude, then all the more reason to throw a spoke in the wheel. They would find him not so easy a mark as his brother. *He* would not be hoodwinked by a couple of scheming females. Moving to the window he scowlingly watched the little hussy report to the other two.

Tonia was comically describing the silent contest, and, despite the gravity of the situation, both Julia and Colin had to laugh at her audacious behaviour, a reaction that their observer found disconcerting.

"Well, let us try to puzzle it out," Tonia suggested. "From what you have said, Colin, I am led to believe that this is somewhat out of character for your brother?"

"Where I am concerned it is. Though I *have* seen him fly off at others in the past when something upset him."

"There must be some extraordinary factor involved," Tonia decided. "Did he say anything that would account for his unreasonable stance?"

Colin looked at Julia protectively and confessed, "He has been to Atlee Hall. He and the earl arbitrarily decided that I should marry Atlee's daughter. They are coming to Glenview next week to settle it."

"Aha! So that's it!" Tonia announced triumphantly. "He is going to be made the fool, and it rankles him. I presume that is not a role he would play willingly?"

"No. And I have never known him to allow himself to be put in such a vulnerable position," Colin told her.

"Well, he will certainly be in a box when Robert and Emily arrive," Tonia commented.

"Robert and Emily?" Colin queried with raised brows.

"The earl is Tonia's most persistent suitor," Julia revealed with a laugh.

"Oh, Lord!" Colin exclaimed, breaking into a wide grin. "This has all the makings of a farce."

"It is certainly a good beginning," Tonia agreed. "But let us take first things first. Now, what do you think of this stratagem?

49

We will all pretend to accept the duke's dictum. And then we will just casually mention that Julia has a sizeable fortune of her own, letting him know that you will not be destitute."

"Yes. And we can discuss the prospect of your accepting employment from Father, as he is in fact prepared to offer," Julia proposed, throwing herself into the game.

"Marvelous, Julia," Tonia approved, nodding her head.

Colin looked at them in amusement and added, "I will tell Derek that, unless he has serious objections, we will remain at Glenview until my mother comes—" And so three irreverent conspirators devised plans to flummox the duke, with expressions of increasing hilarity as Colin came to recognize the absurdity of the situation and soon regained his natural self-confidence.

From his lookout Sayer was glumly experiencing a foreboding that he might have to eat humble pie before this was over, since the forces working against him obviously had little respect for his eminence. But he would not give in easily, he fumed, as he glared malevolently at the small figure whom he identified in his own mind as the architect of this unhappy state of affairs.

Learning that his aunt was still napping, the duke retired to his suite, which he had installed for himself in a remote corner of the castle several years before in order to have some semblance of privacy during his short periods of residence. His stepmother had never really reconciled herself to a relinquishment of her former rights and often came with her husband and sometimes her friends to spend several weeks.

The Earl of Merrill was an agreeable, easy-going person who felt secure enough in his relationship with his wife to be disposed to allow her her little postures. However, he had seriously discussed his lady's presumptions at Glenview Castle with Derek. He did have sufficient authority over his wife, when he chose to use it to insist that she recognize her stepson's ascendancy and stop treating the castle as though it were still her domain, neither waiting for an invitation nor announcing her impending visits. But Sayer had brushed aside the earl's apologies, not thinking the matter important enough to create a stir, and instead had just had the private apartment prepared for himself.

By the time the duke had conferred with his butler and his housekeeper and had bathed, shaved, and changed from his dusty riding clothes, Lady Alvinia had already risen and joined the others in the drawing room, where she had been immediately apprised of the amazingly incredible *contretemps* that had taken place a few hours before. She received the story with considerable scepticism, not admitting that Derek, who was a particular favourite with her, could be capable of such abominable behaviour. But after hearing the whole of it again and observing the lingering expression of hurt in Colin's eyes (though, guided by the girls, he had brought himself to a realisation that the situation certainly would right itself in time), she had come to understand that the duke had indeed acted insupportably.

"Under the circumstances, you three look remarkably undaunted," she said curiously.

"Oh, but we have conceived a plan," Tonia informed her with a glint in her eye. "We have concluded that the duke must not suppose that Colin is in any way put to grass." And she revealed the strategy they meant to employ to convince him of the folly of his ways. "Will you help us?" she asked.

"Certainly not!" Lady Alvinia declared emphatically. "I refuse to be any part of this conspiracy."

"But surely you cannot approve the duke's actions," Julia protested as she reached for Colin's hand, prepared to champion her beloved.

"No, my dear, of course not. But I am sure Derek will come to his senses without these provocative machinations."

Colin was enough pained by his brother's ill-conceived burst of temper that he was not adverse to dealing him a measure of retribution, so he sided with the girls in their aggressive posture. "Will you at least not give us away, Aunt Alvinia?"

Shaking her head, realizing this promised to be just one of many abnormal diversions during the coming weeks, his aunt agreed. "All right, Colin. I just hope you know what you are doing. Derek has a fair measure of pride, you know."

"So do I, for that matter. I will not be spoken to as though I were a grubby schoolboy!" Colin said adamantly.

A few minutes later the duke entered. With a studied composure he crossed the room to greet his aunt affectionately.

"Derek," Lady Alvinia said, with a soft light in her eyes, "how good it is to see you. We have been waiting for you. May I introduce you to Colin's fiancée, Julia, and her sister, Miss Antonia Radcliffe?"

Though Colin's admonitions still angered him, the duke nevertheless played his proper role as host and gentleman. Bowing to the two ladies, he said, "I am pleased to make your acquaintance, Miss Julia—and Miss Radcliffe."

Julia smiled artlessly and responded with an easy charm, "Thank you, your grace. I have been so looking forward to meeting Colin's brother"—an innocent remark that prompted the duke to say to himself, "I don't doubt you were!"

Bridling at the cynical look on his face, Tonia merely nodded her head. "Do you not speak, Miss Radcliffe?" the duke enquired.

"When the occasion calls for it, your grace," she replied.

"And have you not also been looking forward to making my acquaintance?" he asked.

"Perhaps I was, at that," Tonia allowed, with a deprecative smile, seeming to apologize, prepared to take immediate advantage. "It was only a natural thing, you see, as Colin was so disposed to sing your praises."

Lady Alvinia, putting her hand over her mouth to hide a smile, felt almost sorry for her nephew, pitted against this redoubtable girl who meant to make him squirm.

In truth, it took all the duke's self-control to receive this sally with any measure of equanimity, but he privately had to admit his error in setting himself up, though he determinedly suppressed the sense of guilt the jibe had evoked.

Impressed by Tonia's opening thrust, Colin moved to offer his support of their scheming, and he addressed his brother with a natural affability that he was yet far from feeling.

"Derek, notwithstanding our being at odds on a particular matter, I hope you will countenance our presence here until Mother arrives. I expect her imminently; I don't doubt she too has her prejudices and will jump to conclusions. I would divert her if I knew just where to send a message, but I'm confident she is en route. However, if you feel it would be better for us to leave before your guests arrive, we will return immediately to Dunstable."

My God, thought the duke. So I am to be drawn and quartered. How the devil did I dig this hole for myself? Aloud he only said, "Don't be a numbskull, Colin. Of course you may stay."

"Very well," the younger man acknowledged. "We will leave as soon as all is resolved, since I will be anxious to take up an occupation."

Refusing to be routed, the duke enquired sceptically, "And what are you prepared to do that will bring you enough to support yourself and your wife?"

"I never realized what a poor opinion you had of me, Derek," Colin observed with a wry expression. "As it happens, I have a particular challenge in mind. When we were at Julia's home, I became very much interested in her father's work, and he jokingly offered me employment should I find myself in need. I never expected to have to call him on it, but now, of course, I have every reason to, and I am coming to find the prospect an exciting one." Ignoring the duke's fascinated stare, he continued, "Mr. Radcliffe is compiling notes on the Napoleonic wars, so I was able to help him there. In fact, I told him you too would be a good source of information for him, and *he* is anxious to meet you. I hope you will one day invite him to Glenview."

"And this is your proposal for supporting a family?" the duke scoffed.

Deciding it was time for her to speak her piece, Julia told him gently. "It will not be very lucrative, perhaps, your grace, until

Colin builds a reputation like my father's. But that really does not matter, you see, since I am possessed of a comfortable fortune myself."

I suppose I must consider it a blessing that there are only three of them, the duke thought ruefully. He had no recourse, that was apparent. Lord! He only hoped Robert had not done too good a job of persuading his daughter. He would let them come, he decided. The girl was young, after all, and certainly could be brought to reason if she had in fact set her heart on this connexion.

Realizing that he had not acknowledged Julia's words, he brought himself to attention and remarked deliberately, determined to play the game a while longer, "Since it seems you are all set, there is nothing more to discuss, is there?" With that he excused himelf, saying that he would rejoin them at dinner.

The three confederates were tolerably well satisfied with the first round. At least they had made the duke accept the fact of Colin and Julia's betrothal. These two wandered off to the garden, and Tonia remained with Lady Alvinia.

"Tonia, I don't doubt you initiated this unmerciful campaign," the older lady chided lightly.

"Something had to be done, Lady Alvinia, as you would have agreed had you seen the look on Colin's face this morning. He was absolutely crushed. It had never once occurred to him that his beloved brother would treat him with such contempt. I had to try to make light of it. And I thought if I could help him find some measure of relief from the weight on him, it would be all to the good."

"It just seemed that you were all enjoying Derek's discomfiture a bit too much. But I suppose, given the provocation, it would be unrealistic to expect the three of you to hold yourselves in check. How long do you propose to turn the knife?"

"I don't know," Tonia replied thoughtfully. "We will see what develops."

At dinner the knife went several inches deeper as the ruthless threesome enlarged on Colin's prospects.

"Papa will be so delighted," Julia enthused. "He has never really gotten over the death of our brother. He had great plans for them to work together. And you know that those hours you spent with him gave him a great deal of pleasure, Colin."

"You had a brother?" Lady Alvinia asked.

"Yes," Tonia replied. "Mark—after Marcus Aurelius, you know. He was three years younger than I—your age, Colin (a side comment the duke found very informative). He was killed in Spain in '11."

"What a waste," Lady Alvinia sighed, "like so many others."

"Yes, Aunt Alvinia," the duke agreed. "But some must go to fight, and some of those are fated to be unlucky."

"Why did you say 'after Marcus Aurelius', Tonia?" Colin asked.

"Oh," Tonia laughed, revealing alluring dimples, "during the years when we three children were born, Papa was very much interested in Roman history. Marcus Aurelius had always been his favourite emperor, so naturally he saved that name for his son. At the time I came into the world, Marc Antony was in favour, but, by the time Julia was born, Papa had come to the conclusion that my 'patron' had been something of a ramshackle character and felt obliged to give Julius Caesar his due."

Even the duke was forced to show his appreciation of this whimsical history. Tonia noted that he had a very pleasing laugh, which made her think perhaps he might not be so bad after all.

Deciding he had better remove himself from this Machiavellian group before he ended up giving his blessing prematurely, the duke withdrew immediately after dinner. The conspirators, being deprived of their target, contented themselves with more commonplace games and soon retired to their rooms.

=6=

WHEN TONIA AND Julia were sitting alone at breakfast the next morning, an early visitor was announced by Nestor. The baroness swept in with an expectant look on her face that caused Tonia to burst out laughing.

"Alicia, the duke has arrived, as I'm sure you are aware, but he is out riding with Colin. However, if you will settle for our company, we would be pleased to entertain you. Would you like some coffee?"

"When will he be back?" the baroness asked as she sat down.

"We don't know, as we are not in his confidence," Tonia replied dryly.

Lady Alicia looked at her sharply. "Surely he has not thrown a spoke in the wheel?"

"He tried to," Tonia divulged with a smug smile.

"Ah, a breach! You must tell me all about it," the visitor said, leaning forward eagerly.

"Certainly not!" Julia said. "It's only that the duke took exception to Colin's and my engagement. But we have convinced him we are firmly committed."

"Is that all you mean to say?"

"Yes. It is, after all, a private affair," Julia declared firmly.

The baroness took this rebuff goodhumouredly; her forward ways had left her open to many such setdowns. "When is Colin's mother expected?" she enquired.

"Very shortly," Tonia answered, "but we have not heard any specific date."

"How typical of the countess. One day she will just appear," Lady Alicia said in exasperation. "I want to hold a ball, and I must give my guests some notice. Well, I shall just set it for next week and chance that everyone will have arrived."

56

"The duke is expecting other guests next week, Alicia, so you might find it expedient to wait until the following week," Tonia suggested.

"Who is coming?"

"The Earl of Atlee and his daughter, Lady Emily."

"In that case I'll hold off until Saturday," the baroness decided. "When did Derek ride out?"

"About half an hour ago," said Julia.

"Well, I suppose I might as well drive into Southwell and come back later. Does either of you want to accompany me?"

"Not I, thank you," Tonia said. "I am progressing nicely on my painting, and I want to get started on it early today. I will likely not have as much time as our numbers grow."

"How about you, Julia?"

"Why yes, Alicia. We have not ventured into town yet, and I can look over the shops for future reference. I will get my bonnet and be ready in a few minutes."

Not long after they had left, Colin and the duke returned, just as Tonia was about to ask a stable boy to help her carry her painting gear.

"Wait one minute, Tonia. I'll help you with that," Colin called as he dismounted. "Where is Julia?"

"The baroness came. When she found she had missed the duke," Tonia told him, purposely not looking at the second gentleman, "she decided to drive into Southwell. Julia went with her, but they will not be too long, I'm sure, for you know Alicia has been very neighbourly, enquiring almost daily for the duke."

The duke did not miss the amusement behind this remark, and he looked balefully at his laughing brother. "I will thank you not to encourage the baroness's visits," he said, speaking directly to Tonia.

"Your grace, I can assure you she does not need any encouragement, for she seems singularly friendly. And since I have no quarrel with her, I cannot think why I should cut her," Tonia replied.

Realizing that doing him a good turn would not be one of Miss

Radcliffe's ruling ambitions, Sayer resigned himself to the necessity of discouraging Alicia himself. Damn the woman. He would have no peace if she meant to persist in casting out her lures.

As he disappeared into the house, Tonia turned to Colin and asked, "How did it go this morning?"

"Quite as if we were on excellent terms," Colin told her. "It was as though yesterday's turnup never happened. Neither of us brought up the subject. We just talked about Glenview and the other properties he visited this spring."

"Then it appears he will relent, as he probably already has in his own mind, though he will have to be beguiled into admitting it," Tonia judged.

"Perhaps. Except that, you know, even if he does keep to his word now, he cannot turn away from the fact that I am still his heir."

"Which is, of course, how he can warrant requiring your company on his rounds," Tonia noted wickedly. "You *do* feel better about it, don't you, Colin?"

"Yes," he answered with a smile, "especially as I know he cannot long resist Julia's charm."

"Of course not," Tonia agreed. "Now do help me set up in this shady spot on the terrace. I am far enough along that I can work here. And," she added, "I should not like to be too far away when Alicia returns."

Colin laughed. "You *are* a mischief, Tonia."

Almost an hour later Tonia heard the light carriage coming up the drive. After a moment Julia and the baroness joined her on the terrace.

"Has Derek returned?" Alicia enquired eagerly.

"Yes, very soon after you left, actually," Tonia said brightly.

Resisting an impulse to take exception to this provocation, the baroness merely threw Tonia a dark look and turned to go into the house.

The other two laughed, and Tonia informed Julia, "I think you will find Colin in much better spirits. It seems the duke has chosen to put aside his dire threats and behave as if there was no problem."

"Oh, I'm glad, Tonia." Julia sighed in relief. "Colin was so dreadfully unhappy. And it was not because he would be denied a portion, you know. But he truly loves and admires his brother."

"I know, Julia. Think how it would be with us. I could not bear it," Tonia declared feelingly, an assertion that earned her a warm embrace from a like-minded sister.

Inside, Alicia had asked Nestor to send word to the duke that she had come to call, and she was waiting impatiently for this gentleman's appearance.

Finally he came with Colin in tow. He greeted her pleasantly. "I must thank you for looking in often on my aunt. I had meant to call on you and the baron in a day or so."

"Oh, Derek," the lady protested, making a face, "do not be so formal." And she attempted to throw her arms about him, but he caught her wrists in his hands and held her off.

With a little pout she announced, "I have been talking with Antonia and Julia about my decision to hold a ball at Ealand next Saturday to welcome all your guests."

"That will be very good of you, Alicia. And later, we will return the courtesy," the duke replied affably.

"It will be lovely to have you home again, Derek," the baroness fairly purred. "It has not been very satisfactory to have seen you so rarely during these war years."

"I shall be spending more time at Glenview now, Alicia," he said. "I have many improvements in mind, and will be extremely busy seeing that they are implemented." Turning casually to his brother, he asked, "Where are the Misses Radcliffe, Colin?"

"On the terrace. Tonia is painting."

"Well, let us go see how she is coming along. I should like to know what sort of painter she is."

The baroness had no choice but to precede them and reluctantly led them to Tonia's corner.

The duke stood behind the artist and looked at the canvas with critical eyes. "Yes, I recognise the spot. You are very talented, Miss Radcliffe."

"Thank you, your grace," Tonia said absently as she applied herself to mixing her colours.

At dinner that evening there was a general unspoken commitment to maintaining a tentative peace, so the conversations did not invite any untoward controversy. And though the duke did not participate in the discussions to the fullest extent, he did make occasional contributions when applied to, and joined them for a while afterwards in the drawing room, remaining until his aunt was ready to retire.

By chance all four young people congregated in the library at the same time the next afternoon. A furious storm had blown up, and outdoor activities were out of the question. The duke gave attention to some business papers, Tonia read the newest novel of Miss Austen, and Colin and Julia played cribbage. After a while, upon Colin's learning that his betrothed claimed to be an expert at billiards, he challenged her to a game, leaving Tonia and the duke alone.

Tonia looked up from her book to see the duke gazing thoughtfully after the departing couple. "They really are very much in love," she said softly. "And their deep attachment is such that I am certain it is no passing fancy."

The duke turned to her and asked speculatively, "How can you be so sure, Miss Radcliffe? They have only known each other a few months."

"Have you no communion with fate, your grace?" Tonia enquired whimsically.

The duke studied her for a moment, considering the question, before he replied, "I'm afraid I do not."

"I cannot think that answer is completely accurate, your grace," Tonia challenged. "Perhaps you mean you do not believe in fate's playing a part in romantic affairs. You certainly appear to have allowed that it has some relevance as regards who falls in battle. Or do you give more credence to chance?"

Although he suspected this discussion was going to lead him more deeply into a morass, Sayer was not being able to resist matching wits with this artful baggage. "I suspect you have hit the mark," he said. "My store of faith cannot be stretched to cover the concept of true and lasting love."

"I see," Tonia mused. "And does your scepticism apply to a lady's capability or to a man's?"

"It has been my observation, Miss Radcliffe, that a lady's affections are easily gained or lost by any number of mundane considerations, none of them being the love of an honourable man."

Tonia looked at him with new interest. "Oh, dear!" she exclaimed sympathetically, "you have had a *Disapointment,* haven't you?"

If a look could have slain her, Tonia would have met her Maker at that very moment. And had she been of a timourous nature, she surely would have withered under the glare of pure malevolence cast in her direction by the incensed gentleman. But since she was not, she returned his glare, as if daring him to chastize her.

"You, Miss Radcliffe," he said cuttingly, "have more cheek than is admirable in a young woman of quality."

"Balderdash, my lord duke," Tonia scoffed. "I really cannot imagine why you have such a crochet about it. It was when you were very young, I expect. Before you went to war most likely— twenty-three, perhaps? What a long time to nurse such an unadmirable obsession! One would think you were the only one who was ever deceived in an affair of the heart," she continued indignantly, under the duke's incredulous gaze. "You are not, you know. Why, *I* have had a disappointment myself. Would you like to hear about it?"

"Do I have a choice?" he asked sarcastically.

Tonia paused and considered for a moment. Having become

very much caught up in this stimulating exercise of bandying words with the duke, she could not quite bring herself to the point of making what in her own mind would be an unsatisfactory, premature end to it. So she said, "Now I could say yes, which would naturally compel you to deny an interest. But since you did not flatly say no, I shall oblige you and take your question as an affirmative answer."

"My God!" Sayer groaned to himself, wondering why he should invite such punishment.

"I was very young, also," Tonia began, "—eighteen—and filled with romantic notions. Eighteen is a very dangerous age for young ladies, you know, especially if they are addicted to romantic novels, peopled with dashing, handsome heroes, as most of them are. And you need not look so knowing, your grace. There is really nothing wrong in harbouring fantasies, particularly if they lighten a dull life and are recognised for what they are. It is true that sometimes one can be misled, as I was. However, in the long run no harm was done, so I can only judge it to have been a worthwhile experience, teaching me as it did, that a gentleman's honour cannot always be trusted."

Tonia remarked the flicker in her opponent's eye, and the slight curve of his lip, which betrayed his appreciation of her thrust. But giving no indication that she knew she had scored, she continued, "He wore a uniform, of course. I *do* think it terribly unfair to females that our officers are outfitted in those highly seductive regimentals. One can be so blinded by their brilliance as not to be able to be properly discerning about who is wearing them."

"You judge a bird by its feathers, Miss Radcliffe?" the duke asked sardonically, as if it were no more than he expected.

"Only from afar, your grace. As I told you, I learned my lesson. And I am come to think—I beg you will not take offence, though, actually, I don't know how you cannot—that the bright uniforms that fighting men have chosen for themselves can only be an extension of their general inclination to peacockery. For if ever men were walking targets, soldiers certainly are in those scarlet coats, a fact that became apparent in our conflict with the Colonies, as Papa has remarked."

"The Americans did not fight honourably," the duke noted sharply.

"They did not fight by your rules, you mean. They fought how they could with what they had for what they believed in. But as I was saying," she proceeded, cutting off further argument, "I was very much taken with my officer and was in transports when he said he meant to talk to my father. Papa did not raise any overt objection, merely asking that we wait a year to marry. I will have to say that I am come to realise that I must not have been all that enraptured, since this stipulation did not seem at all unreasonable to me. I'm sure it should have done were I madly in love. However, the gentleman was not as tractable about the delay. And while I naturally imagined that he was overcome by my charms, I did not feel easy in my mind when he began to speak of eloping. Since I had great respect and consideration for my parents, I discussed my qualms with them. I must always thank Papa for his faith in my own good judgement. Contrary to forbidding me to entertain any further hopes for the connexion, he merely suggested that I look into the matter more carefully. I understood he was telling me without being explicit that my suitor might have ulterior motives, so I put the gentleman to the test—and he failed miserably. He was a fortune hunter, of course, and had come to the end of his rope. It was a dreadful blow to me, especially when he married a wealthy widow ten years older than he within the month."

"And is that why you have never married, Miss Radcliffe?" the duke asked curiously.

"Oh, no!" Tonia denied with a merry laugh. "No, I can assure you, I have many times counted my blessings. Why, I have seen him since, recently, and he is the most revolting creature. No, my lord, I am not averse to marriage. It is only that I am an incurable romantic, I'm afraid, and I just have not found the marvelous thing Julia and Colin have. I do continue to harbour hopes. In fact, I shall tell you, adoring Colin as I do—he is the most exceptional gentleman I have ever met—I was very excited when I learned he had an older brother who was just of an age to suit me, supposing that there would be an agreeable similarity in their persons and characters. 'How lovely,' I thought, 'if we should be doubly connected.' And I have spent many idle hours this past month or so anticipating making your acquaintance."

"I must say, Miss Radcliffe," the duke said, taken aback by this bold revelation, "that you are remarkably candid."

Tonia looked at him as though she did not understand, although in truth she had led him to the brink. Then she declared with intentional indignation, "Oh! Of all the coxcombs! You need not suppose I mean to set my cap for *you,* your grace—you did not heed my words, it is clear. I said I was hoping for an older version of Colin, and I think it extremely high-flown of you to suppose that you in any way compare to your brother."

"Hoist by my own petard, Miss Radcliffe. I bow to your *coup de maître,*" the duke admitted gallantly and with a rueful grin, for some unacknowledged reason almost relishing his defeat.

Tonia was a little surprised by this mild reaction, and decided a retreat was in order. "I can see," she said, "that you have had quite enough of my dissertations, so I will leave you in peace. But, your grace," she added before walking out the door, "whether you like it or not, Colin and Julia are a match."

Sayer almost laughed aloud at this last shot. He shook his head at the departing Tonia and grinned broadly. "What an outrageous little termagant!" he thought. Then he proceeded to take stock of his ridiculously untenable position and once again wondered how he had managed to manoeuvre himself into the uncomfortable role of complete fool. Except for this one time he could not remember ever having behaved in such an improvident, wholly insensible manner. How many bottles had he and Atlee downed that night, he wondered? Even if he had been befuddled then, he certainly was not when they had pursued the matter the next morning. How the devil *had* he arrived at the preposterous conclusion that he had the right to settle Colin's future in the matter of choosing a wife? It seemed totally crackbrained, now he thought on it. Heaving a deep sigh, he roused himself from his humbling contemplations and went to confer with his aunt.

Lady Alvinia's abigail answered his knock promptly and admitted him to her mistress's boudoir, where he found the diligent lady sitting by the window, intently at work on her tapestry.

"Well, I see you are not indisposed, my love. I thought perhaps you might be when you did not come down this afternoon."

"No, Derek. It is just that the day was so dreary, and I always find it particularly easy to apply myself to my needlework at such times. What have you and the others been doing?"

"Julia and Colin abandoned me for the billiard room, and Miss Radcliffe proceeded to trample me underfoot."

Lady Alvinia burst out laughing. "Oh, dear! I know it must put you off to hear me say so, but I positively adore Antonia. It is a long time since I have become acquainted with anyone so much after my own heart."

"From that remarkably unfeeling observation, I must assume you do not propose to offer me sympathy," her nephew commented with a wry grin.

Lady Alvinia smiled affectionately. "Derek, I have not wanted to interfere, because I knew you two boys regarded each other too highly to long remain at odds. But I could hope you would make an effort to swallow your pride and smooth things over. It is your error, as I'm sure you are aware, and you must take the initiative. The thing of it is, Colin did not imagine you would take exception before you met Julia, and certainly not afterwards. But I know he *is* expecting some opposition from his mother. Feeling as I do that he and Julia are deeply attached and eminently suited, I would like to know that you were in their corner before your stepmother arrives."

"Well, my dear, I am happy to tell you that already I have gone that road. I will set things to right immediately." With this happy assurance, he left a well-satisfied lady and went to seek out his brother. Finding him and Julia just hanging up their cues, he asked amiably, "And did Julia prove her expertise?"

"I was thoroughly trounced," Colin admitted with a rueful grin. "I will pit her against all comers."

"Where did you acquire this proficiency, Miss Radcliffe? It hardly seems a usual accomplishment for ladies," the duke observed.

"When Mark was home, the three of us often played, and Tonia and I have continued to do so."

"Is Antonia an expert, also?"

"Well, perhaps not," Julia replied immodestly, "but she is a good loser."

Amid laughter, Derek noted, "That can be an admirable trait on some occasions. I have come to ask if I may appropriate Colin for a little while. I will return him to you shortly."

"Of course, your grace," Julia consented with a little chuckle. "Perhaps you will help him nurse his wounds."

"We shall nurse each other's," the duke told her candidly. "I have just suffered at the hands of your sister."

Seeing he did not appear to be out of temper, Julia did not offer any apology and with an understanding smile left the two men alone.

"Colin, let us go into my study. I have some things to discuss with you."

When they had settled themselves, Sayer made a clean breast of it. "Colin, I wish to offer my abject apologies for that incredibly highhanded demonstration the other day. I can't think what possessed me to lord it over you like that. It was inexcusable, and I can't tell you how deeply I regret it. I must say you have been remarkably charitable about it. I doubt I could have taken it with such fortitude."

A slow smile spread over the younger man's face. "Had I not had a pair of monkeys to counsel me, I might not have either," he allowed. "But, trusting that I had not deceived them about our close relationship, Julia and Tonia persuaded me that there was some unusual twist involved and wheedled me with their arguments into giving you the benefit of the doubt."

"I am forever grateful to them," his brother said sincerely, "for I quickly perceived that you were a better man than I and that it smacked of unwarrantable pretentiousness on my part to presume to instruct you. You obviously need bow to no one when it comes to discernment. Julia is a lovely girl. I wish you every happiness."

"Thank you, Derek," Colin said as the two clasped hands. "I knew you would see how captivating she is once you had met her. I cannot yet believe my good fortune in having won her affection. But, Derek, I still don't understand how this imbroglio came about."

"I have wondered myself. I have even considered that I was in my cups. But I think rather it was my unadmirable obsession that led me astray. I have little sympathy with the concept of romantic love, I'm afraid. Not planning to marry, myself, I felt a compulsion to see you settled and starting your nursery, not knowing that you had the same idea and were already managing very well on your own. So I persuaded myself into playing the matchmaker, thinking that it would be desirable to promote a connexion between the houses of Sayer and Atlee. Damned cheeky, I admit," the duke said ruefully.

"Well, since you have seen fit to retract so promptly and freely, there is no reason to belabour the matter," Colin pronounced generously. "I am content to think no more on it."

"That is very good of you, Colin, though I know you cannot but be offended by my cavalier actions."

"To tell you the truth, Derek, after I left you and had talked to the girls, the whole thing seemed so unreal and out of character for you that I never actually believed a word of it. Though I have to say I found it hard to stomach that you had the gall to mouth such fustian, even in a moment of clouded perception."

The duke threw back his head and laughed. "All right, Colin. I can tell you I was not all that amused with being reminded of my youthful folly in such graphic terms, either. But we will wipe the slate clean. I have been corresponding with our solicitor these past few months to discover just how much of the estate I am free to turn over to you outright at this moment. The properties in Cheshire and in Essex are not part of the entail, so I have directed him to proceed in drawing up papers to transfer ownership immediately. In addition, I will sign over half of the assets invested in the funds. I feel obliged to keep the rest of the estate intact. The other holdings, except for Glenview, are not now self-supporting. I will have to keep something in reserve to cover any unexpected setbacks."

"You need not apologize, Derek," Colin said with his slow smile. "I knew you meant to be generous, but I did not expect so much. In good conscience I feel I have to remind you that it is entirely possible that I might not always be your heir and that you are substantially depleting your resources."

"I don't think you need concern yourself with that, Colin. There is still more than enough. And besides, what is gone before one hears of it can hardly be missed. When are you and Julia planning to be married?"

"In September. I thought by then everything would have been resolved. But if Mother comes round quickly, we will likely make it earlier. You will like Julia's family, Derek. Her mother and father are an exceptional couple. And of course Tonia is a diamond."

"I can see that you two exchange an immoderate admiration. I have it in the lady's own words that you stand extremely high in her eyes and that she had been looking forward to meeting me in hopes that I might be an older version of you."

"Good Lord! Did that minx tell you that?"

"Yes. But she also confessed her disappointment and was quite emphatic in her admonition that I need not be puffed up because, as it turned out, I am not at all of your quality."

"That will teach you to set her back up by trying to cut me down," Colin warned, laughing heartily.

"Well, I can tell you that I mean to be particularly careful not to do so again. I find I am not in any way equal to the contest. Now," the duke said as he tugged at the bell pull, "let us send for Miss Julia. I wish to mend my fences with her."

Julia was with Tonia in her room when she received the summons, and she looked questioningly at her sister.

"He was overmatched, love," Tonia hinted with her impish grin.

"You are a disgracefully wicked girl," Julia accused with a giggle, throwing a well-directed pillow before hurrying to learn what had transpired.

Sayer welcomed her, "Come in, Miss Julia. Colin and I have made some dispositions, and since you are concerned, I wish to tell you what we have decided. First, though, I do humbly beg your pardon for my abominable behaviour. I have no excuses, but I do most sincerely offer you my best wishes and will tell you that I am very happy Colin had the good sense to exercise such excellent judgement in his choice of a bride."

"Your grace—"

"No, no—it is Derek. I am to be your brother, you know."

"Yes, of course." Julia put her hands on his shoulders and kissed his cheek. "Thank you, Derek. I am very pleased that you and Colin have resolved your differences."

Colin then sat her down and disclosed how far he had come from being a penniless suitor. She listened attentively, smling at his boyish enthusiasm. "You will be very busy with all your responsibilities," she teased him. "Papa is going to be terribly disappointed."

"No, I will do that, too," Colin promised.

"I will leave you to your plans," Sayer said in amusement, and left the room, knowing he would not be missed.

Before the party gathered downstairs, Lady Alvinia and Tonia had learned that all was well. They both conveyed to the duke their approval of his action and expressed their delight that Colin and Julia were to be so well situated.

During dinner it was apparent that Tonia and the duke had called a truce, and the lively conversation covered a wide variety of subjects. The duke informed them at one point, "I have heard rumours that Newstead Abbey is to be put up for sale."

"I thought it might be," Colin said. "It would be the only way for Byron to resolve his financial difficulties."

"I have considered making a bid for it. What do you think of the idea?"

"I'm not sure. There are a great many acres involved," Colin replied. "If you did acquire it, it would certainly make up for what you are turning over to me."

"Aren't there rumours of ghosts in the Abbey?" Julia asked.

"Yes," Lady Alvinia confirmed. "It is said the Black Friar walks just before some disaster is to fall. Byron claims he saw this spector prior to his unfortunate marriage to Miss Milbanke."

"Well, if that isn't a far-flung excuse for his poor showing as a husband, I don't know what is!" Tonia declared indignantly. "Why, it is beyond anything."

The others laughed and agreed that it did seem a lamentably shabby means of justifying a desertion of family responsibilities.

7

THE NEXT MORNING the entire household gathered to go into Southwell and attend Sunday services at the ancient Norman minster. Their arrival at the church was remarked with interest as they took their places in the front pew, which had been reserved for the Neville family for generations. It had not often been occupied these last several years, as Lady Alvinia only occasionally came to services. However, on those Sundays when she did not, the minister, who was her old and cherished friend, came to Glenview to perform a short private ceremony in the castle's chapel, usually remaining for luncheon and an intimate gossip.

After the service the party from Glenview was obliged, in effect, to form a reception line. Many of the townspeople and some of the families from the surrounding estates pressed to pay their respects to Lady Alvinia, who was familiar to everyone since she had been a resident of the neighbourhood longer than all but a few of them, and to welcome the duke and his brother back from the wars. They were eager, as well, to be introduced to the two beautiful young women who had come to visit Glenview.

Leaning on the duke's arm, Lady Alvinia held court. She had a special word for everyone, being truly interested in the people in her generally narrow orbit. Julia and Tonia were regarded frankly, and their natural amiability easily created a favourable impression. It was known, of course, that Julia and Colin were to be married. And as might have been predicted, some of the more romantic-minded dowagers and impressionable young girls let their imagination persuade them that another match could not be far off. Two young ladies and their mothers claimed a special connexion with the Misses Radcliffe by reason of having met them at various affairs during the London Season. They were quick to call on this fact to extend invitations to their homes, which both girls graciously accepted, even while hoping there would be some way of disentangling themselves from the obligation.

The duke unexpectedly came to their aid by announcing that he must ask that the ladies be excused from making calls for the moment, as he was expecting several more guests and very much feared the entire household would be fully occupied within the boundaries of Glenview for a while. "However, as soon as we are settled in for the summer, we will hold a grand ball and welcome you to the castle."

With this extravagant and tantalizing promise to mollify them, the petitioners did not press their invitations, though they went away hoping to encounter their "friends" on some chance occasion.

Alicia, with her husband, stood waiting for the crush to thin out. Finally, losing patience, she effectively dispersed the rest of them. The baron, a white-haired man, yet younger in appearance than Tonia had expected, grasped the duke's hand and said sincerely, "Welcome home, Derek. I have been watching with considerable curiosity the changes you have instructed your steward to initiate, and I am awaiting the results with interest. I would appreciate your explaining the methods more fully when it is convenient."

"Gladly, John. I will be more than happy to. Scientific farming has become one of my pet projects. Why don't you and Alicia dine with us tomorrow evening so we can discuss it?"

"Thank you, Derek. We accept with pleasure," the baron replied, knowing his wife would mount no objection. Being well aware of her ambitions, he had long since reconciled himself to her "infidelity" which, because of her exclusive obsession with the Duke of Sayer, remained purely imaginary. For that, he actually considered that he owed the younger man a debt.

Clouds were beginning to form, and the Glenview party judged it expedient to return immediately to the castle to try to avoid a wetting. A few drops were just beginning to fall as they pulled into the courtyard, and they hurried inside, congratulating themselves on having handily circumvented one of Nature's caprices. After removing some of their finery they gathered again for luncheon in the small salon near Lady Alvinia's chambers.

"Derek," Colin said, "why don't we take the girls on a tour of at least part of the castle today since it appears we are going to be housebound? We haven't begun to explore yet, and I know they are curious, being inveterate history enthusiasts."

The duke agreed promptly. "Where shall we start?"

"The state apartments would be a good place," Colin suggested.

"Come, ladies," said the duke. "I shall unmask our splendours. The state apartments are rarely used and serve mainly as a setting for some of Glenview's treasures. However, first we will show you the *pièce de resistance*." He led the way down to the ground floor and opened a door off the main hall to a long corridor leading to a flight of stairs at the end.

"The castle is very large, though not so extensive as it once was. Part of it was damaged during the Uprising and then was razed after the Restoration. My father hired an architect thirty years ago to make a survey of the entire structure, giving him a general concept to work with and letting him make the necessary improvements. You see, a castle is not the most comfortable dwelling. But rather than abandon the ancestral hall that had been the home of the Neville family for hundreds of years, he decided to renovate a section of it to make it liveable but to preserve its antiquity as much as possible from the outside and in the old wings that would be merely repaired. The center section of approximately thirty rooms we have modernized and redecorated to serve as our living quarters. The state apartments were also restored, though more particular attention was given to maintaining the original purpose and style of each room. But first we will go into the Great Hall," the duke said as he opened a heavy oak door and stood back to allow the ladies to enter. "It is the only room in the keep that we have maintained, and it is the only remaining chamber to have been used since the castle was first built in the fourteenth century."

The room was immense, with a beautifully timbered forty-foot roof. On both sides toward the far end were high windows, and tapestries hung the length of the hall. At one end there was a minstrel's gallery and at the other, an enormous fireplace with the family coat of arms mounted on it.

"It is magnificent," Tonia said in an awed whisper.

"Yes," Colin agreed. "It is the most impressive room in the castle. I came here often as a boy and in my mind I used to recreate some of the scenes that I imagined had occurred here."

"Yes," the duke confirmed, "whenever we missed Colin, we always knew where to find him."

In the newer section of the castle, where the state apartments were housed, Derek escorted his guests through the state dining room, drawing rooms and bedchambers, all of them elegantly furnished. "These rooms are maintained by a special group of servants who are assigned to keep the furnishings in good condition, closing the draperies so the sun will not fade the tapestries, upholstery and carpets, and checking for signs of deterioration in general," the duke said.

"It is really an expensive obligation to preserve such a heritage, isn't it?" Julia asked dubiously.

"Yes," the duke agreed, "it is. Fortunately a lot of work was done fairly recently, so with reasonable care it should not be too much of a burden."

On their way back to the main apartments they stopped to admire the small, elegant family chapel, with its stained glass windows on the west wall above the altar. It had been built four hundred years ago and, after years of neglect, had been faithfully restored by the present Duke of Sayer's grandfather.

By this time the skies had cleared and there was a bright sun shining, so they went outside for a continuation of their tour. "We will be able to see a good part of Nottinghamshire from the Tower," Sayer told them. "We are centrally located here with an extended view in all directions."

After they had admired the varied surroundings from their lofty perch, they carefully descended the curving stairway and then walked to the walled section, following the ramparts into a corner block which had served as a guard post. After the rains it was damp and musty smelling, so they did not linger long. "Now," the duke concluded, "you have seen most of the castle, though there are other areas we have locked up because they have become malodorous and dangerous. Much of the old section must be torn down as it has long since served its purpose and has become an eyesore and a health hazard."

"Your grace—" Tonia began as the tour was concluded.

"Antonia," the duke said, "I do wish you would dispense with the formality. We are friends now. I would rather have you address me by my given name."

"Well, then I shall," Tonia replied, "though how you could act as though I should have done so before, when this is the first I have heard of it, I'm sure I cannot imagine."

"My error again, it seems," he murmured with an unusual glint in his eye.

With the distinctive smile that gave her the appearance of a mischievous child, Tonia made her request. "My lord—Derek— I would very much like to see the place you have chosen for hanging Lady Alvinia's tapestry."

"I must apologise for my brother's negligence. It seems you have been accorded only minimal hospitality. Come," he said, offering her his arm, "we will do that now. You can see the room from here. It is a long gallery on the east wall. My apartments are just above it."

The foursome entered the room and were immediately struck with its great length. "Here where these portraits now hang is where I thought the tapestry would be displayed to best advantage," Derek said. "What do you think, Antonia? I would appreciate an opinion."

"Yes, I think that would serve very well. This is a beautiful room for the purpose," Tonia said. "Derek, is *that* truly a Raphael Madonna?" she asked in awed tones, moving to stand before a prominently displayed canvas.

"Yes," the duke replied. "It is our masterpiece."

"Oh, how exquisite! There are other excellent works here, but this is superb. If ever *I* should be missed after a time, you will know where to find me. I may set my easel up in here some day and try my hand at copying the Madonna."

That evening, as they all spoke easily before dinner with the baron and Alicia, Tonia mused to herself, "Why, the baron is a very charming gentleman. Alicia should count herself extremely lucky. I can't think what she is about to behave so insensibly. It is positively shocking the way she is making sheep's eyes at Derek." To becloud this obvious pursuit, Tonia began to devote herself solely to the baron, and they were soon deep into a conversation discussing the merits of several artists whose works were displayed in the annual exhibition at the Royal Academy in the spring. Learning that he had purchased one of Turner's seascapes, she expressed a desire to see it the night of Alicia's ball.

"You need not wait so long, Miss Radcliffe. If you will ride over some morning, I will be pleased to show it to you."

"Then I shall certainly do so," Tonia told him.

"And in return, I hope you will allow me to see your work. I have heard you have a considerable talent," said the baron, a request to which Tonia agreed with a smile that the baron found extremely disquieting.

"What are you two talking about so seriously?" the duke asked as he came to join them.

"Oh, Baron Ealand and I have discovered a common interest. Did you know that he has purchased a Turner?" Tonia said enthusiastically.

"No, I did not. But I must compliment him on his choice. I am determined to have one myself," Sayer told them.

The butler announced dinner, and the party of eight (Reverend Dodson had been invited to join them) proceeded to the dining room.

Despite Alicia's attempts to monopolize the duke's attention, he subtly directed his remarks to include others and soon began

76

to speak of the matter that had prompted this invitation. After some minutes of a discussion of farming between the two men, with frequent interjections from Tonia, Alicia burst out, "Derek, for heaven's sake, could we not speak of something that would interest the rest of us? I have heard quite enough about farming!"

"Of course, Alicia. I will beg your pardon," the duke said with a sheepish grin. "I become very voluble when I get started on this subject, I'm afraid. We gentlemen will continue our discussions after dinner. Now what would you like to talk about?"

"Well, for one thing, tell us about the Duke of Wellington. Is he as much the ladies' man as rumour has it?"

"And *that* is what you want to know about the duke?" Derek asked in mock-dismay. "Here we speak of one of the greatest generals, greatest men, in fact, that has ever lived, and you ask a question like that!"

"Derek—is he?"

"Yes, as a matter of fact," he admitted reluctantly.

"And were the balls and festivities in Vienna truly glorious?" the baroness asked eagerly.

"Yes, Alicia, but I was not there very long so do not ask me to elaborate."

"I mean for the musicians to play several waltzes at my ball this weekend. Colin, I do hope your mother arrives in time, else I may be in her black books."

"Well, there are five days yet, so do not give her up. I expect her myself."

It was time for the ladies to retire to the drawing room, leaving Colin, the duke and Baron Ealand to their port. Lady Alvinia retrieved her cane and headed the procession of ladies to the formal salon.

"I do hope they are not too long," Alicia remarked ill-humouredly. "I think this custom is positively gothic."

"Well, as they often use the opportunity to smoke their nasty tobacco, I for one am glad they do it in private," Tonia pronounced.

It was not long before Colin and the Reverend Dodson rejoined the ladies, and Lady Alvinia and her good friend promptly retired to a corner to continue their game of chess.

The continued absence of the duke and the baron predictably threw Alicia into a huff. "Do they mean to ignore us for the rest of the evening?" she complained.

"Very likely," Colin said. "They were deep into the matter of crossbreeding when we left."

"I will not have it!" Alicia declared furiously. "John has no right to monopolize Derek and keep him from his other guests."

"You forget, Alicia, that Derek invited your husband just so they could compare notes on farming," Colin remarked.

"They can do that some other time. Do go bring them to us, Colin," the baroness pleaded.

"Alicia," he said in some exasperation, "put a damper on it. Good Lord! If we have to put up with your throwing yourself at Derek all summer…"

"How dare you speak to me in such an impertinent manner!"

"Because you invite it, Alicia. But if you don't stop making a fool out of yourself and embarrassing Derek, you are in for a surprise. I can tell you he will not suffer your stalking him much longer. One would think after fifteen years you would realise he is not interested."

The baroness stood up in fury. "I will not listen to your insults another minute," she stormed and she flung out of the room, ordering a footman to see that her carriage was brought around.

Colin looked at Julia and Tonia sheepishly, saying, "Not a very gentlemanly performance, was it?"

"As you say, she does ask for it, Colin," Tonia reassured him. "Her single-mindedness does become something of a bore. I wonder the baron countenances her behaviour."

"Well, she is really not a bad sort, as her type goes. And he does not worry about her making advances because, as Aunt Alvinia has said, he knows Derek will not take her up on it."

"It is too bad she behaves so shockingly when the baron seems to be a very good man," Julia noted.

"Yes, he is well liked and respected by the neighbourhood, and, if truth be known, by Alicia as well. Though she may mouth offhand remarks when he is not around, you may be sure she does not do so to his face."

Finally the other gentlemen came out of their den with apologies for having delayed so long. On learning that his wife had left earlier, the baron did not request an explanation, having a fairly good idea of what had precipitated her action. He promptly took his leave also, accepting a ride in Reverend Dodson's carriage.

Derek looked questioningly at the others when they were alone, and Colin confessed to being the culprit.

"I am glad you warned her, Colin. Perhaps that will save me the trouble of having to be more specific. I am determined not to let her cut up my peace when I am in residence here. I wish John would take her in hand!"

=8=

WHEN TONIA AND Julia entered the morning room two gentlemen looked at them in surprise.

"So early, love?" Colin asked, rising to kiss his betrothed.

"I rarely sleep late, Colin," Julia told him with a smile. "Tonia and I have always been early risers."

"I must say that rather lays bare one of my illusions about the female sex," Derek commented.

"One of your many," Tonia interposed with asperity.

The others laughed, but the duke persisted, "You will allow it is not the usual thing for ladies to appear bright-eyed at seven in the morning."

"That depends," Tonia said, once again tempting her adversary toward another quagmire.

"On what?"

"On whether or not they have something to do, which, I grant you, many do not. And while I hesitate to make such an injudicious observation, your grace, I do question your source of reference on the subject," Tonia said, looking at him with an expectant expression and daring him to elaborate.

"Tonia!" Julia exclaimed blushing while Colin laughingly admonished his brother, "You will learn not to leave yourself open like that, Derek."

"I had better," the duke remarked blandly. "It is a pity you have made prior plans," he said to the ladies. "Colin and I are riding out in an hour or so to inspect some of the fields and to speak with the tenants. We would have welcomed your company."

"Did I say I had other plans?" Tonia demurred quickly with a surprised look.

"I thought you said you had something to do," Derek

hazarded, knowing full well she would concoct some totally unanswerable riposte.

"Well, yes, but that is not precisely the same thing as having plans. In a general sense I always have something to do," Tonia told him amiably.

"Antonia, if that means that you would like to accompany us, I wish you would say so," Derek said in exasperation.

"Well," the shameless lady hesitated, perfectly satisfied with this exchange, "I shall have to ask Julia."

"Oh, yes, Tonia, let's go. I should enjoy it," her sister exclaimed.

Turning to the duke, Tonia said, "So! Let that teach you not to throw invitations out so casually."

"My education is being broadened daily," Derek allowed with a rueful smile. "I wonder what trap I will trip next?"

"Perhaps you did not really mean..." Julia began doubtfully.

"Do not let him off so easily, love," Tonia protested hastily. "He is much too opinionated and unversed in the ways of ladies. It is our duty to him and to our sex to school him."

"Colin," the duke asked with an air of sufferance, "are you fully prepared to take on this little virago as a sister-in-law?"

"Of course, Derek," Colin responded with a grin, having listened to the foregoing dialogue with much amusement. "I told you. I am one of Tonia's many captives."

"Ah, I forgot," Derek acknowledged with a wry face. "Well then," he added, turning to Julia, "we would be greatly pleased to have your company this morning. The tenants and workers will be glad for the opportunity to become acquainted with Glenview's lovely guests."

"Thank you, Derek," Julia said with a sunny smile. "We will be no trouble, I promise you."

On this warm summer day, Tonia and Julia dressed in their new lightweight riding habits, fashioned with empire bodices, rather full skirts trailing in back, and trimmed in braid on the sleeves and up the fronts. Their hats were round and small brimmed, with moderately high, barely tapered crowns. The duke was quick to notice Tonia's changed appearance when her hair was tucked away under her hat. She looked even smaller and younger, yet more sophisticated, and her green eyes were more striking, reflecting the bright emerald of her costume. Julia, too, with her lighter hair and blue eyes, looked lovely in her sapphire habit.

The gentlemen helped the ladies mount, and then the four of them rode out towards the fields. The farming acreage was not visible from the castle grounds because of the well-planned plantings, designed to give the impression of endless park-land. However, beyond the wooded area, the extensive fields, thick with wheat and other crops, also seemed to stretch endlessly. In a very few minutes the riders came to a fence. Colin dismounted and unlocked a gate, allowing the others to pass through. On one side there was another fenced-in area where cattle and sheep grazed.

"What do you raise here, Derek?" Tonia asked with interest.

"A variety of things, not always the same every year. We are experimenting with different crops. But a good part of our profits come from our sheep."

They could see workers in the fields, which were neatly divided by hedgerows, and there were wagons loaded with hay.

"Where do the tenants live?" Julia inquired, looking around for signs of habitation.

"In scattered areas. But we are rebuilding most of the cottages and have several stonemasons working constantly. Some families have moved into new homes. We held a lottery to determine who was to get them. Eventually all the tenants will live in a village-like setting near the river," the duke told her.

Tonia and Julia lagged back when the two men dismounted to talk to some of the labourers, who acknowledged the ladies' presence with a self-conscious touch to their hats. After a time, the two men returned, and Derek said, "Come, now, we will ride down to inspect the new housing."

They could hear sounds of building as they neared the site, and, presently, on the other side of a small grove of trees, there appeared several stone cottages, each with a little ground for a home garden around it.

"Oh, how charming," Julia exclaimed.

There were little children playing, chasing each other, causing a great deal of confusion. Several young matrons took time out from their duties to pay their respects to the duke and his brother and to catch a glimpse of the beautiful ladies. Derek spoke to each of them and introduced his guests before leading the way to the new school that had been completed in his absence.

"Derek," Tonia said, as they rode side by side on their way back to the castle, "I must commend you for providing an education for the workers' children. It is so very important for them to be prepared to make their way in the world."

"Yes, I am hoping that all of the youngsters will learn some trade or profession. Now that steam engines are being developed and there is a new interest in machinery of all kinds, fewer hands will be required on the farms. Besides the school to teach reading and writing and other scholastic subjects, I am forming another institution for practical studies. Some of the men who served with Colin and me are going to teach manual arts like blacksmithing, carpentry, bricklaying, stonecutting, and such. I intend to extend the service to children of families on my other properties and give them the opportunity to come here to apprentice for a while."

"Derek, that is a truly worthy project," Tonia applauded with a speculative look in her eyes. "I begin to see what Colin meant."

The duke looked at her questioningly, and she smiled as she explained candidly, "Oh, when I asked if you were like him, he said that you were a character unto yourself and that he knew no one *quite* like you. And I have to agree to the extent that I have never before met a man of property who showed such concern for his people."

"Then," Derek remarked significantly, "you also are a proper candidate for a broader education in the ways of the opposite sex."

"So it appears," Tonia granted with a laugh.

After they returned to the castle, Tonia changed clothes and was about to enter the drawing room to join Lady Alvinia when she heard a commotion in the lower hall. She moved to the head of the stairs to look down, instantly being witness to the arrival of Derek's invited guests.

"Ah," she thought mischievously, "now for the next act." She began to descend but stopped halfway until the earl and his daughter were welcomed by the duke. Then she continued down the stairs and was almost at the bottom when the earl looked up and saw her.

"Tonia?" he said in bewilderment. "Tonia?" He put his hands over his eyes and murmured, "It is true I have been thinking of Tonia, but surely I could not conjure her up before my very eyes—"

"Robert, don't be absurd," the amused lady admonished as she laughed and went to take his hands.

"Tonia, what are you doing here?"

"Well, my lord, I'm afraid this is going to come as something of an unwelcome surprise, though it wouldn't have if you had been in London for the Season for then you would have seen it develop. Julia and Colin have formed an attachment and are going to be married."

"Good Lord! And after all our well-laid plans!" the earl exclaimed with a wry face as he looked at his friend who merely shrugged his shoulders and gave a resigned sigh, finding it hard to fathom just what was going on. These two seemed remarkably well acquainted.

Tonia withdrew her hands and turned to speak to the young girl who was standing by with an equally bewildered look on her face.

"Emily, I am very pleased to meet you. I am Antonia Radcliffe."

"*You* are Miss Radcliffe?" the pretty, dark-haired girl asked incredulously.

"Yes, my dear," Tonia replied with amusement. "Am I not as you expected?"

"No. I mean—I thought—well—that you were older."

"You must tell me some time how you gained that impression," Tonia said, throwing a dark look at the earl.

"Oh, no," the girl said in confusion. "It's just that I thought you had had many Seasons."

"A *good* many, in fact," Tonia admitted, "for I am twenty-nine."

"You don't look to be twenty-nine," Lady Emily told her.

"Thank you, my dear. I can see that we are going to be great friends." Tonia took the girl's hand and spoke in a confidential tone. "Now, I must tell you that your father and the duke have been extremely unwise to have raised your expectations in a certain matter. You see, my sister, Julia, and Lord Neville met in London and fell instantly in love. It was quite the most beautiful thing—like a fairy-tale romance. You must ask Julia to tell you how it all came about. Then you will know not to settle for such an indifferent arrangement as was planned for you. Not that I think you will not fall in love with Colin. I'm afraid you might, for he is a most exceptional gentleman. I am extremely fond of him myself. But, unfortunately for the rest of us, my sister has captivated him. So you and I will just have to find someone else."

Lady Emily giggled and said, "Miss Radcliffe, you are a complete hand."

"Well, you know," Tonia advised with a twinkle in her eye, "we must learn to accept these little setbacks with good grace and put them behind us so that we do not let them direct and unduly influence our relationships with others forevermore." Having thrown out another philosophical tidbit for whom it might concern, she was confident that it would hit the mark, as it did indeed, much to its target's amusement.

She continued, "I can't think what your father was about, that he could have been misled by the duke into such an insensitive, arbitrary decision about your future," casting a reproachful look at the earl who stood with a bemused expression on his face. "Of course one might look for such an inconsiderate posture from his grace who, you understand, does *not* believe in romance. But I would have expected the earl to be more thoughtful. However, it is clear that the matter must be taken out of their hands. Why, you are just out of the schoolroom and have not even been presented! I cannot believe you would not wish at least to look about for yourself. And in that regard, a lovely idea has just occurred to me. But we will discuss it in private. Come. I have kept you standing here too long. You will be wanting to refresh yourself." And putting her arm through Emily's, she said, "When you have rested for a while, we will have a long talk and afterwards go to find Julia and Colin, who no doubt are hiding in some flowery bower," eliciting another delighted giggle from her charge.

Both the duke and the earl stood watching the two figures until they disappeared up the winding stairs. Then they looked at each other and burst out laughing.

"So it has been since I came home," Derek remarked ruefully. "I have absolutely no control over anything that goes on in this house. Miss Radcliffe is a damnably managing female."

"Well, you will have to admit she got us out of a hobble rather prettily," the earl told him.

"She did at that," Derek agreed. "Let's go to my study. I will explain the matter."

"I thought Tonia made it perfectly clear," the earl said.

"You know the beginning and the end. The in-between is what put me in Miss Radcliffe's black books, though I expect, from the moonstruck look on your face, you did not notice those little darts thrown in my direction." Observing his friend's sheepish smile, he asked reluctantly, "Tell me, Robert, is *that* little devil the woman you told me you have been languishing for these past five years?"

"Yes, Derek," the earl confessed, not quite registering his friend's provocative description. "I have been in love with her since we first met."

"And I have had to put up with your bearishness these past months because you would have rather been in London dancing attendance?"

"That's right," Atlee admitted with a wide grin.

"Well, for God's sake, why didn't you say so?" the duke exploded.

The earl rose and walked over to look out the window. "I have proposed several times, you know, and she has always refused. I thought she might have come to take me for granted. So when you asked me to accompany you, I did so, hoping she would discover that she missed me. I think perhaps she did. At least she seemed to be reproaching me for not being in London." Turning back to his friend, he said with a twinkle, "I must say I think it extremely accommodating of you to have snared her for me."

The duke could not bring himself to view the matter in quite the same light, telling himself that he could not wish such an uncomfortable female upon his good friend, rather than admitting to any other reason for his antipathy to the match. Putting this disturbing contemplation in the back of his mind, he began to tell the story of his doltish exhibition and then described the manoeuvrings that led to his unconditional surrender.

"Good Lord, Derek," the earl exclaimed incredulously, "how the devil did you let yourself make such a piece of work of it?!"

"God only knows. I can only be gratified that Colin was persuaded by his mentors not to take me seriously. In any case, all is well now, especially since Emily is being enlightened by your friend. However, I'm afraid our peace will be short-lived, since we will likely have another imbroglio when my stepmother arrives."

"When is she coming?"

"Any day, I expect."

Both men then spoke of other matters, though it must be said that neither would have been given high marks for attentiveness, both seeming to be distracted by more pressing issues that preoccupied them.

It absolutely beat all, Derek mused, how an otherwise perfectly intelligent man could show such a total lack of attention to a sense of self-preservation when enamoured of a woman. Robert obviously had rats in his upper storey to have thrown his hat over the windmill for Antonia Radcliffe. It *was* true, Derek conceded, that she was a well-looking female. And she *did* have a rather delightful, whimsical way about her that was entertaining. But surely Robert must see that she was not at all in his style. Why, in a trice, she would ride roughshod over him, and he would end up being merely a cat's paw. He was much too nice a fellow to be condemned to such an ignominious fate. *That* vixen needed a strong hand that could keep her on leading strings. And with these promptings from his subconscious, the duke handily convinced himself it would fall to him to make his friend realize that, so far, he had been saved from landing himself in a hornet's nest and that he should not be so buffleheaded as to spin Fortune's wheel again.

The earl's thoughts, while they centered on the same fashionable lady, contrasted markedly with the duke's. He envisioned lovely scenes of strolling with her in the gardens, perhaps sharing an intimate picnic with her in the little temple and of once again declaring himself, with every hope that she would at last make him a happy man. Had he been aware of his friend's unpropitious deliberations, he would have taken strong exception to his intention to meddle. And perhaps, from having experienced competition in a variety of guises these past five years, he might well have entertained some ominous suspicions. But since both gentlemen elected to conceal their inharmonious contemplations, their inevitable face-off was happily postponed.

While Emily was changing from her travelling gown and having her hair redone by her maid, she marvelled that she should meet Antonia Radcliffe in this peculiar fashion. She was familiar with her name, of course, for she had been aware for some time that her father hoped to marry her. He had not been the least evasive about it, having on occasion expressed his intention to introduce the two of them. And she had often wondered about the woman who had caught his fancy. But never in her wildest imagination could she have pictured such a fascinating lady. She felt a faint chagrin that she had not visualized her father as a romantic figure—one who would pursue an Incomparable. It did not seem so strange now she thought on it. He was only thirty-nine and still a handsome man—and a good catch, she had heard it said. She had been misled, of course, by her conception of Miss Radcliffe as a middle-aged spinster. What a distorted impression *that* was, Emily thought as she let out a little giggle. "Do hurry, Abby," she said, impatiently shaking her curls. Throwing up her hands the maid resignedly put down the brush, once again frustrated in her attempt to represent her charge as a polished young lady. Perfectly satisfied with her reflection in the mirror, Emily hurried to Tonia's room to announce that she was ready for their *tête-à-tête* and was all of a flutter to hear about Miss Radcliffe's "lovely idea."

"Well, it is this," Tonia began. "You see, for the past six years Julia and I have gone to London together and so have had each other to share things with. But next year she will be married, and our situations will naturally be different. So I hope you will allow me to be your sponsor and present you next spring. I'm sure we could persuade your father."

"Oh, Miss Radcliffe! Would you truly?" the girl exclaimed, clapping her hands. "I would like that very much. And I will confess to you that I *was* a little disappointed when Papa told me of his plans."

"Well, I would think so! You are a lovely girl and will certainly be a belle. We are going to have a famous time. And I think you may call me Tonia as we are to be friends. At dinner we will tell the earl what we have decided. Now let us go find the lovers. You will adore Julia."

"And Lord Neville, too?" Emily asked impishly.

"Yes," Tonia answered with a merry laugh. "But remember, you can't have him."

Emily giggled and followed Tonia out into the garden. They continued down the terrace until they neared the river where they finally spied their quarries sitting on the beach with fishing lines in their hands.

"I know it is not the thing to interrupt anglers," Tonia called gaily, "but I have brought a guest to meet you."

Julia and Colin turned around and immediately drew in their lines. They picked up their catch and walked up to meet the newcomers.

"Well," Tonia chided, "I must say you two have rather confounded my representations. I have been telling Emily we would come upon you in some idyllic setting, and instead we find you toting a basket of malodorous fish. Emily, my dear, may I introduce you to my sister Julia and to Lord Colin Neville?"

Pleasantries were exchanged without embarrassment as it was immediately apparent to the betrothed couple that Tonia had taken the matter in hand and had neatly cleared the air.

"Julia," she said, "I have promised Emily that you would tell her how you found your true love, a man of your very own choice, so that she will understand such things really *are* possible and will not allow herself to be drawn into any such scheme as her father and the duke invented in their own muddleheaded way."

Colin grinned. "Something tells me my hapless brother has suffered another setdown at your hands, my dear Tonia. Welcome to Glenview, Lady Emily."

Looking at this blond giant with the engaging smile, Emily felt a twinge of regret. She glanced conspiratorily at Tonia. "I see what you mean, Miss Radcliffe—Tonia."

"Yes, I thought you might," Tonia said ruefully, "but I *do* hope you will restrict yourself to fantasies."

Emily burst out laughing and accepted Julia's invitation to walk back to the castle with her so they might become acquainted. "Tonia is right, you know," Julia instructed as she linked arms with her companionably. "You must not suppose that everyone should settle for an arranged marriage. And you are so very young to be relegated to the role of matron."

Colin strolled by Tonia's side and asked for a report of her resolution of the matter. She gave him a rather complete account, and he commented, with a faint suggestion of reproof, "I hope you know what you're doing, you little mischief."

"What do you mean?" she asked innocently.

"You know very well what I mean. I am aware you intend to bring Derek to heel. But I beg you to remember that he is very vulnerable when he bestows his affections. I would not like to see him made game of again."

Tonia was silent for a moment, a little disturbed by this not entirely justified accusation. It was true, she conceded, that she felt a continuing strong impulse to make the duke eat humble pie. His poor opinion of women was not to be borne! However, as far as Colin imagining his brother susceptible, surely he was putting a false construction on the matter. Derek was not just another vulnerable male. Besides, she was perfectly confident that with her experience she would know where to draw the line to avoid landing herself in the briars. So she assured smoothly, "I promise you I will not hurt him, Colin."

"All right, Tonia. I will trust you to hold to your word."

They all entered the castle in high spirits and stopped at the drawing room to present Emily to Lady Alvinia. The duke and the earl were there, and Robert immediately offered Colin his congratulations.

"Thank you, Robert. Since you are well acquainted with Julia, you know how lucky I am."

"Yes, Colin, I do. And I hope you will not hold my part in this folly against me. Derek and I were way out of line."

Lady Alvinia suggested, "Derek, I think it would be best if we did not publicize this regrettable bobble. It would serve no purpose but to titillate the gossips. Does anyone but those of us here know of your ill-conceived proposal?"

The duke raised his brows and looked at Atlee and Emily.

"I haven't mentioned it to anyone," the earl said.

"Neither have I," Emily answered, but then added uncertainly, "except to my maid."

Colin let out a laugh. "So much for keeping it quiet. Might as well have announced it from the Tower."

"I doubt it matters," Derek decided, "so long as we show a solid front now." He well understood that his aunt was afraid Colin's mother might be very much taken with what might have been.

To celebrate the arrival of two honoured guests, dinner was to be a festive occasion. Dressed in new gowns, Julia and Tonia drew frankly admiring glances from the gentlemen when they entered the drawing room together, for the light silks hung closely and clearly revealed their lovely forms.

Robert came immediately to appropriate Tonia and led her to the couch, sitting next to her with an air of familiarity.

"Now, my dear, tell my if you missed me," he teased.

"Of course I missed you, Robert," she answered unaffectedly. "I got myself in all sorts of trouble because you were not on hand."

"You do, even when I am," the earl noted ruefully.

Later, at dinner, Tonia informed the earl about the matter she had discussed with his daughter. "We have decided that I will chaperon Emily next spring in London and introduce her to society properly. I told her I was sure you would agree."

"Oh, yes, Papa. There is no one I would rather have as a sponsor," an excited young lady vowed with sparkling eyes.

"That is a generous offer, Tonia," the earl said, not at all averse to such an arrangement. "If you would not find it an imposition, I would very much appreciate your taking on the business."

"So! There! It is easily settled," Tonia concluded. "We will go to town a little early and buy all manner of lovely things."

"You had better be prepared to lay down the blunt, Robert," Colin advised with a laugh. "Tonia is notorious for the money she spends on clothes."

When they had all gathered in the drawing room after dinner, the earl took the opportunity to speak privately with Tonia. "My dear, I have been chastizing myself regularly these past months for having passed up the chance to be with you in Town. I can't imagine how I let Derek persuade me to chase all over England instead."

"Well, Robert, it is perfectly understandable," Tonia assured him reasonably. "It was good to renew your friendship, since he had been away for so long."

"Yes, so it was," the earl admitted. "But I did miss you. And I had planned to come to Dunstable after I left here. However, I find this felicitous encounter much more satisfactory."

"Robert—" Tonia said warningly, not meaning to let him forget how things stood between them.

"I know, Tonia," he acknowledged with a wry face. "I won't make you uncomfortable."

This little *tête-à-tête* was observed by the others with varied speculations. Lady Alvinia felt a curious apprehension, having hoped for a particular development. She had been watching Derek and Antonia move cautiously towards an understanding, perhaps without being aware that they were doing so. But there had been little doubt in her mind but that these two would eventually make a match of it. And now suddenly this complication had arisen with the arrival of the earl. She had not realised quite how much she favoured the connexion until she saw it threatened. She hoped Derek would soon recognise his feeling for Antonia for what it was and seriously throw his hat in the ring.

The duke himself was experiencing a peculiar uneasiness. He should have prevented Robert's visit, he thought ruefully, since their scheme had proven entirely in error. Instead, he had thrown his friend into the little temptress's path once again. The fact that Tonia could have easily snared the earl anytime these last five years escaped him for the moment. He only knew he took strong exception to the appearance of intimacy between the two of them.

Lady Emily, approving her father's aspirations, entertained lovely thoughts of having such an exceptional stepmother, and Julia and Colin, unaware of all these varied estimations of the same subject, had their own convictions. Being better acquainted with the situation, they made resolutions to help Tonia keep the earl at bay.

=9=

THE NEXT MORNING Tonia was determined to get back to her painting. She gathered her materials and slipped away early, while the three men were out riding, telling only Julia where she was going. Lately she had found herself experiencing a nagging feeling of restlessness that she found curiously discomfitting. She could not quite identify the source of this anxiety and finally attributed it to being denied the privacy she had been accustomed to after the hectic London Season. Except that she was beguiled by the lovely settings that cried out to be put on canvas here at Glenview, she could almost wish for the peace and quiet of Dunstable, so that she could pursue her work without being distracted by all these complicated personal relationships which threatened to become awkward.

Because of the unpredictability of the weather she chose a spot near the little temple so that she could run for shelter if it should come on to rain again. She asked that one of the young stable hands be summoned to drive her to the lake in a small work cart. When everything was set up, she directed, "If it begins to rain, Tom, come back for me right away. Otherwise, I will expect to see you in three hours."

"Yes, ma'am," the boy replied respectfully.

She then settled down to work, soon becoming totally absorbed in transferring the scene before her onto the canvas.

When the men returned from their ride and joined the rest of the household, the earl immediately enquired for Tonia and was sadly disappointed to learn that she had expressly instructed that she not be disturbed. Derek, however, found this intelligence entirely acceptable, admittedly pleased that his friend was thwarted in contriving a rendezvous. The night before, as he lay awake in bed reviewing the day's events, the duke had begun to suspect that his determination to cool the earl's passion for Tonia might be inspired by ulterior motives. And once he had gotten that far, it did not take long for him to realize that he was fairly caught himself. "This is a pretty kettle of fish," he thought in dismay. Was that miserable female a sorceress in disguise? It was incredible that even the most hardened bachelor, like himself, should so easily succumb to her charms. So? Did he mean to play the gentleman and leave Robert a clear field? Certainly not! And that was an indication of the depths to which he had fallen. With every intention of keeping track of the earl, Derek invited him to accompany him to Nottingham to make some purchases for his steward. "We will take the greys and make a fast run of it," he said as a temptation.

Colin and Julia had offered to give Emily a tour of the castle, but after an hour of wandering through dark halls, they decided they would rather take advantage of the beautiful weather. So they begged a picnic basket from the kitchen and walked down to the river to enjoy a day of warm sun and gentle breezes.

When Tonia returned to the castle, she found all quiet, and she wondered where everyone had gone. While she was changing from her old gown and was washing the paint off of her fingers, a maid came to tell her that Baron Ealand had called, asking if she would see him.

"Of course, Sally. Please tell him I will be down in a few minutes." Now what could he want? Tonia wondered. Perhaps he just wished to leave a message. She dressed hurriedly and then went down to the salon.

"Good afternoon, baron."

"Good afternoon, Miss Radcliffe. I hope I did not disturb you."

"No," Tonia said with a smile. "I was just trying to make myself presentable after my painting session this morning. I'm afraid I am not very neat when I work.'

The baron laughed and told her, "I am on my way back from Southwell. I hoped to be able to persuade you to come to Ealand Hall with me. I would like your opinion on the Turner and on some of my other paintings."

"Why, thank you, baron. It is very accommodating of you. I will get my bonnet and be ready in a moment," Tonia said not realizing that she was inviting yet another difficulty.

A few minutes later she was being handed into a handsome curricle by a very pleased gentleman who had been a little dubious about his chances for carrying her off. The baron, still under fifty, did not have a roving eye, but he was well aware that he found Antonia Radcliffe extremely fetching. And, given his wife's indifferent attentions, particularly since the object of her longtime passion had come home, he saw no reason to deny himself the pleasure of seeking the company of another woman who could share some of his interests, a lucky circumstance that gave him an excuse to see her without putting either of them in an embarrassing position.

"Do you have any pressing engagements, Miss Radcliffe?" he asked as he drove leisurely down the drive.

"No, I don't believe any definite plans have been made for the afternoon. Everyone seems to have scattered. The house is deserted, except for Lady Alvinia, who always rests at this time."

"Then I will not hurry. The day is unusually felicitous and perhaps will give us a respite from the daily showers," he said with a smile as he looked at her with pleasure.

"Yes, a very attractive man," Tonia mused admiringly. And then, in sudden realization, having had years of experience in observing wistful males, she groaned to herself, "The devil! Surely not! Really! Antonia, how do you get yourself into these hobbles?" Resolving to keep the situation in hand, she tactfully turned the conversation to the subject that prompted this excursion, and soon the two of them were genially exchanging impressions of the styles of several contemporary artists.

They pulled up in front of a large, new, Greek revival mansion, and the baron took Tonia's arm to escort her into a lovely, intimate reception hall. He enquired of his butler, "Is Lady Alicia in the house, Sibley?"

"Yes, my lord. She came in a few minutes ago and went upstairs to her chambers."

"Will you send word to her that we have a guest and that we will await her on the veranda? And please have some refreshments brought to us."

"Yes, my lord."

Tonia was looking around interestedly, admiring the baron's taste, for she was sure he made final judgements on any acquisitions. He led her into an elegant drawing room and through open French doors to a covered porch that extended the length of the building and overlooked a formal garden with a long reflection pool.

"We will wait until Alicia joins us," he said. "Then I will take you to the library where I have my best paintings."

They did not have long to wait before the baroness came sweeping out the door in her usual brisk fashion. "Tonia!" she exclaimed in surprise.

"I stopped by Glenview on my way back from Southwell to see if I could persuade Miss Radcliffe to come for a visit," her husband informed her. "I thought it would be a good time to show her the Turner. And since she was alone, she agreed to accompany me."

"Where is everyone else?" Alicia asked curiously as she served the lemonade that was brought by a maid.

"Well, I don't really know," Tonia admitted. "I slipped out early to work alone. By the time I returned, the castle was deserted. Did you know that the earl and Lady Emily have arrived?"

"Yes, I had heard. Is she a silly little schoolgirl?" Alicia asked.

"No, I wouldn't say that. She is young, but I find her quite charming and very pretty. I have offered to sponsor her in London next Season."

"Isn't that rather a sudden development?" the baroness remarked, not particularly pleased with Tonia's description.

"Not really, Alicia. Robert and I have been good friends for years," Tonia said comfortably.

"I see," her hostess said speculatively.

"How are things coming along for your party this week-end?"

Tonia enquired, changing the subject. "Do you need any help?"

"Thank you, Tonia, but I don't think so. It is not all that large an affair."

"Even if it were," the baron noted teasingly, "she wouldn't need any help. When it comes to entertaining, no one is as well organised as Alicia."

"Thank you, John," the pleased lady said with a fond expression.

What is this? Tonia speculated in surprise. She had gleaned the impression that Alicia was indifferent to her estimable husband, but it did not seem so today. As this provocative speculation raced through her mind, she heard Alicia maintain, "And to preserve that precious reputation, I had better keep my appointment with Cook. Do you mind if I desert the two of you? I'm sure I would be out of my depth anyway when you begin discussing perspective, masses, impressions, brush strokes and all that sort of thing."

"We will excuse you, my dear," the baron responded. "But perhaps you will join us later if we can tempt Miss Radcliffe to stay for tea."

"Oh, *do* call her Antonia. We are going to be practically living in each other's pockets, and all that formality is quite tedious," Alicia expostulated as she left them abruptly.

Tonia laughed and remarked, "She certainly has an extraordinary store of energy."

"Yes, she always has had. And I am of a mind to follow her direction if you have no objection. Though I shall insist that in return you must call me John."

"Very well, John." Tonia set down her glass of lemonade and rose to walk with him into the house.

When Derek and Robert returned from their trip to Nottingham, they looked about for signs of life and finally came upon Lady Alvinia sitting on the terrace with her little terrier at her feet.

"Well, my love, are you deserted?" Derek asked whimsically.

"For the moment," his aunt replied. "Julia, Colin and Emily will be back in a few minutes. They just came up from the river where they have been picnicking. The wind turned them into a pack of tousle-heads."

"Where is Antonia?" the earl inquired. "Surely she is not still at work?"

"No, I believe she came in just after lunch. But she has gone to Ealand Hall. Nestor said the baron came in his carriage and invited her to go with him."

"My God!" Atlee exclaimed expressively. "Not another one!"

"Relax, my friend," Derek told him with an amused expression. "They were discussing John's new Turner the other evening at dinner, and she expressed a desire to see it."

The earl grinned and admitted, "I've become a little jaundiced, having spent the last five years competing with Tonia's other conquests."

"Are there that many?" the duke asked harshly.

"Good Lord, Derek, you must be blind! That woman has refused more offers than she can count."

"Is she a practiced flirt then?" the duke said angrily.

"No! It's just that—well, dammit, man, you have to admit that she is a very seductive looking lady."

The duke said softly, "I grant you that."

"And the rest of it is that she is just naturally unaffected, intelligent and disposed to friendliness, besides being interested in people and having a great deal of wit, all of which puts her in a class of her own and attracts men like a magnet."

"My God!" his friend groaned. "How can a man of your age and general good sense stand there and mouth such inanities! That paragon you have just described bears about as much resemblance to Antonia Radcliffe as one side of a coin does to the whole. Even if she *could* be credited with all those attributes that you enumerated, that is not by any means the rest of it. She also has a Machiavellian mind, which she uses unmercifully, always fights for the upper hand, is damnably managing and on top of that is deliberately provocative."

"Tonia?" the earl asked incredulously. "You must be mad. I know you don't have a good opinion of women in general, my friend, but this time you have gone off half-cocked. And I will thank you not to broadcast those prejudices," he continued belligerently, "lest we—"

"Robert," Lady Alvinia intervened, having listened to this heated discussion until she thought she would burst from trying to hold back her laughter, "do come to your senses. You merely have divergent impressions of the lady. And I have to tell you that Derek's viewpoint is not entirely groundless. Tonia made things very hard for him after he set up her bristles by playing the *Grand Siegneur*. He is still smarting."

"I must apologize, Lady Alvinia," the earl said sheepishly. "I'm afraid I forgot myself."

"What was all the shouting about?" Colin asked as he came out on the terrace with Julia. "You sounded as though you were about to come to cuffs."

"Robert took exception to some of my opinions about a certain lady," Derek told him, looking at Julia with laughing eyes. "But Aunt Alvinia has commanded us to meet halfway, so it is done."

Emily came to join them then and asked immediately, "Where is Tonia? I haven't seen her all day."

"She is visiting at Ealand Hall," her father informed her. "She should be back soon."

In fact it was more than an hour later that they heard a carriage approaching. The earl went inside to intercept Tonia in the entrance hall. "Tonia, I can't believe that this whole day has gone by without my seeing you. Is that a way to treat an old friend?"

"Now, Robert," she chided, as he led her out onto the terrace, "considering that you had already left the house before I came down to breakfast, I hardly think you can lay the blame at my door."

"Always the upper hand," the duke murmured, looking at his friend significantly.

Robert threw him a baleful look and said to Tonia, "Well, I can see that I shall have to camp at the bottom of the stairs in the morning to catch you bright and early."

"I beg you will not," she protested laughing. "Where was

everyone today? When I came in after lunch, the castle was like a mausoleum."

After the other reports were made, Tonia spoke of her own afternoon. "The baron has some excellent paintings. I was very impressed. Alicia joined us for tea and was full of plans for her ball."

"A ball!" Emily cried excitedly. "When?"

"Saturday night," Tonia told her.

"Does she know we are here?" the girl asked eagerly.

"Yes, my dear, she does. And of course you are invited," Tonia reassured her.

"Oh, how famous! Will there be waltzes?"

"Yes, Emily, but *not* for you," Tonia announced firmly.

"But Tonia! It is only in the country," the young lady wailed.

"So it is. And there will no doubt be top-lofty ladies present, whom we will meet in London next spring, who would be only too happy to cut down a young girl who promises to be the Season's belle. And as to that, you had best start practising minding my strictures lest I change my mind."

"Tonia, you are not going to be a bear?" Emily protested.

"No, my dear, I am not. But I *do* know the rules, and you will have to learn them."

The others listened to this conversation in amusement, and the earl spoke to his daughter sternly, "Emily, I warn you to mind your steps, for I will brook no insubordination."

"Oh, all right, Papa," the girl promised reluctantly.

A few minutes later the group broke up to go dress for dinner. Tonia and Julia opened their connecting door so they could talk. After Tonia bathed and was dressing, she asked, "How are you and Emily getting along?"

"Very well. That was clever of you to tempt her with a Season. But I have a feeling you are going to have your hands full. How was *your* day?"

"Productive and interesting. I made a good start on a new canvas, and I discovered that Alicia is not all that indifferent to her husband. This passion she has for Derek must be something of an obsession—from not being fulfilled or from being a habitual state of mind. It is insupportable that she should continue to be allowed to irritate and embarrass Derek, hurt and humiliate her husband, and make a complete ass out of herself, while making the rest of us uncomfortable. I really think we should do something about it!"

"We?" Julia said quizzically. "I rather got the impression that *you* were well on your way."

Tonia laughed. "I didn't realize it until this afternoon, Julia. And while I really disapprove of that sort of thing, I *am* tempted to stir the coals. If she weren't so sure of the baron, she might think twice about giving him cause."

"Do you think you could keep it in hand?" Julia asked dubiously.

"Yes. I will not actually encourage him, but I won't send him about his business either. Then it will only need that someone whisper in Alicia's ear to make her aware."

"All right, Tonia," Julia said with a shake of her head. "I just hope she doesn't murder you."

"But I will be perfectly innocent," Tonia protested in mock-indignation.

Julia threw up her hands and followed her sister downstairs.

During dinner there was a lively discussion about what should be planned for the next day. Finally Emily prevailed, begging to go to Newstead Abbey since it was so close and since Julia and Tonia had not been there, either. "It is so vexatious that I shall never see the wicked Lord Byron. At least I could visit his home," she declared ardently.

"Emily," the earl admonished severely, "I wish you will not be so thoughtless when you speak. You are merely repeating gossip and know nothing about it."

"I'm sorry, Papa," the chagrined young lady said. "It's just that at school we heard things and always imagined him as—well—a wicked baron like in the romantic novels."

Her father looked at her dubiously and said to Tonia, "Are you sure you want to take on this unruly child?"

"We will do just fine, Robert. Don't forget I was once a young girl myself."

"And addicted to romantic novels," the duke offered provokingly.

"Just so," Tonia acknowledged, showing her dimples.

=10=

WHEN THE MEMBERS of the household gathered at eleven the next morning to visit Newstead Abbey, the skies were still heavy after a long night of storms, and the threatening outlook put a damper on their enthusiasm. However, it was remarked that since it had been raining part of almost every day, they would never make any excursions if they were going to be so poor-spirited as to let a little wetting deter them, and several voices were raised in favour of setting out.

Since these dauntless sentiments were expressed unanimously by the ladies, the gentlemen could hardly show themselves less stalwart. So, in proper attire, the men with their Wellington capes and the girls with their heavy, hooded mantles, the six of them mounted their horses and in a venturesome mood rode towards the east gate of the estate. After continuing on about two miles beyond the boundaries of the duke's domain, they arrived at the entrance to the Byron property.

They spent a little over an hour wandering about the grounds and the gardens. The dreary day proved an opportune time for exploring ruins and hearing tales of ghostly inhabitants. Emily was happily satisfied to have had her gothic fantasies substantiated, and was totally unreceptive to any attempts by her companions to characterize the poet in a less than legendary light.

At the first signs of precipitation, they turned hurriedly toward Glenview to try to avoid being drenched. As it happened, it was an exercise in futility, and by the time they dismounted in the castle yard, they were well served for their foolhardiness. Their wet cloaks were handed over to two footmen for refurbishing. Then they all retired immediately to their rooms to try to repair the considerable damage that had been done to the rest of their toilettes.

When they had made themselves presentable once again, Tonia and Julia started back downstairs. Just as they reached the first floor landing, they saw Derek standing in the lower hall as though he were awaiting someone. At that moment the door was opened by Nestor, and three people dashed in from the rain which had become quite heavy.

With a sudden movement Derek assumed a wooden stance, hands clasped tightly behind his back. He looked every bit the imperious duke as he viewed the newcomers, who were making a noisy show of removing their wet cloaks, with two ladies exclaiming unhappily that surely their shoes and gowns must be ruined.

The younger one, a beautiful, statuesque blonde, dressed in a bright-coloured, rather impractical close-fitting travelling gown, flashed a brilliant smile and walked directly to Derek, murmuring familiarly, "Derek, I am so happy to see you. It is wonderful that you have finally come home." And she put her arms around his neck boldly to kiss him.

The gentleman, however was not disposed to receive this greeting with a proper appreciation. If he had not been so angry, he might have shown at least a token civility. But as it was, he had an unworthy desire to turn the party out, bad weather notwithstanding. He pulled away from her unceremoniously and set her aside so abruptly that she almost lost her balance, having to grab hold of a near sidetable. He merely said coolly, "Hello, Cecily."

Without a word of welcome he turned to the other lady. With a grim expression he requested curtly, "Carla, before you go upstairs, I would like to speak to you in my study."

The newly arrived Countess of Merrill looked at her stepson reproachfully, considerably nettled by this remarkably uncivil greeting. Bristling up, she was about to decline the peremptory invitation but thought better of it when she realized, from the tight-lipped look on his face, that Derek definitely had his back up. So she decided to brazen it out. Placing her hand on his arm affectionately, she agreed, "Oh, *yes,* my dear boy. I *very* much want to speak to you, also. I have been at my wits' end ever since

I received Colin's utterly *afflictive* letter. I *hope* you have been able to repair the damage. How *could* you have permitted him to behave in such a harebrained manner!? Who *is* this girl? We must *do* something."

Having an uncomfortable premonition, Derek looked up to see Tonia and Julia standing back on the shadowy stair landing, interestedly witnessing this little tableau. Their presence made him even more ill-humoured, especially since Tonia had the audacity to grin unsympathetically as she bowed her head and extended her hand as if to say, "It's all yours," before she took Julia's arm to lead her back upstairs.

They heard the duke admonishing the countess brusquely. "We will discuss this in private, if you please. We do have guests here. Charles," he said, putting out his hand, "it is good to see you. Will you join our conference? Nestor, please have a room prepared for the Countess of Falmouth." Then, without further comment, he strode purposefully to his study and held open the door for his stepmother and her husband.

As soon as they were private, he demanded, "Carla, what is Cecily Mervyn doing here?"

He looked so forbidding that Lady Merrill realized at once she had grievously misjudged what his reaction would be. She replied with an air of pretty uncertainty, "But Derek, naturally I *invited* her. You *know* I often bring friends."

"Since when is Cecily a friend of yours?" he inquired ruthlessly, surprising even himself with his unnatural lack of deference.

"Why, I have *always* been fond of Cecily," Lady Merrill answered defensively, feeling obliged to lower her eyes, as she had *not* always felt kindly towards the younger woman. "When we stopped in London to rest for a couple of days, I met her at my sister's. Cecily charged me to scold you for not going to London and to tell you that she was impatient to see you. As we talked, it became apparent that she had not yet made plans for the summer, and since I knew she was a favourite of yours, I conceived the happy idea of asking her to come with us!"

Exercising great self-control over his strong desire to shake his stepmother violently, regrettably a totally unacceptable exercise, Derek narrowed his eyes and said unequivocally, "Cecily is *not* a favourite of mine, as you well know and, if I remember correctly, were once pleased to discover." Looking at the earl, he asked with a scowl, "Couldn't you have scotched this caper? Surely you knew how it would sit with me."

Lord Charles made a wry face as he admitted, "I didn't find out about it until it was too late, Derek. I'm sorry, but Cecily's bags were loaded and she was in the carriage before I knew anything. I'm afraid there was a little dissembling involved."

Coming to a sudden decision, Derek softened his expression but announced firmly, "Carla, in the past, while I was away a good part of the time, I did not object to your treating Glenview as though you were still mistress here. But this time you have gone too far. I don't know exactly what you hoped to gain by this manoeuvre, though I am sure you did have some purpose. But, whatever it is, I can tell you it won't come off." Taking a deep breath, he determined to go the rest of the way. "I hope you will not be hurt by what I have to say, my dear, but we may as well set the record straight from this moment. Now that I have come home to stay, I mean to exercize my prerogatives. So that there will be no misunderstanding, I will state my case clearly. The crux of the matter is that, in the future, I hope you will remember that this is *my* home and that I reserve the right to invite my guests. You will always be welcome with Charles, of course. But I should like advance notice of when you intend to come and of whom you might wish to bring with you. It may not always be convenient for me to have people popping in at any time."

"Derek!" Lady Carla exclaimed in hurt bewilderment. "How *can* you speak so? You have always been such a dear boy. Whatever has put you in such a temper?"

"I'm afraid you did, Carla," Derek told her bluntly. "But in any case it was time for us to come to an understanding."

With tears in her eyes Lady Merrill looked miserably at her husband and pleaded, "Charles, darling, do try to reason with

Derek. It is too bad of him to fly into a huff for *such* a little thing. *Surely* he cannot mean what he says."

"Yes, my love, he does," Lord Charles informed her unpromisingly. "I told you, you remember, when we stopped that first night, that you had gone beyond the bounds. I did not approve, particularly when you were distressingly underhanded about it. Now you must accept the consequences. It is as Derek says, Carla," he admonished gently, taking her hands in his. "He is the Duke of Sayer, and you are the Countess of Merrill. You will just have to accept that as a reality now."

"Oh, I don't know *how* the two of you can be so unfeeling!" Lady Carla declared pettishly, letting tears run down her cheeks, as she began to pace distractedly about the room, genuinely upset by this unexpected, adverse turn of fortune, "when I am at all sixes and sevens with this oversetting indiscretion of Colin's. Here you are *badgering* me about a simple little mistake on my part when my son has let himself be hoodwinked by some— some unsuitable mushroom! I *hope* you are going to tell me that you have brought him to his senses, Derek."

Having a guilty memory of his own initial reaction, her stepson refrained from taking issue as he wished to, merely commenting cryptically, "I rather think you should not prejudge, Carla. It can create unnecessary difficulties."

Lady Merrill stopped short and turned to look at him in dismay. "Derek, *surely* you have not encouraged this regrettable folly!"

"Carla, these past two weeks I have come to know Julia Radcliffe well. And every day I am more and more convinced that Colin has made a marvelously admirable choice. They are perfectly suited and love each other very deeply. I wish you would at least wait until you have seen them together before you form an opinion."

Having already formed an opinion, the lady was not inclined to follow the duke's advice. She began to pace once again, assuming a tragic air as she lamented, "I thought I could at *least* count on *you* to help me scotch this affair. It has been a great consolation to me that you and Colin have been so close throughout the years, as I know you always have his welfare in mind and carry a great deal of influence with him."

"Not as much as I used to, Carla," Derek told her with a wry grin. "Colin is his own man now, and we are become even greater friends. I am come to fully respect his right to direct his own life. I am afraid, my dear, you are going to find us *both* out of harness."

Feeling very much incensed at the duke's uncooperative attitude, Lady Merrill determinedly aired her objections, revealing her considerable prejudices. "Colin *cannot* marry so far beneath him. The girl is merely a country upstart. There has been no title in her family for generations."

"How do you know?" Derek asked curiously.

"I have investigated, of course," Lady Carla replied without elaboration. "Colin could look much higher. It is not to be thought of that he connect himself with a schoolmaster's daughter."

"That description is not precisely accurate, though I should credit it as no particular obstacle if it were. Matthew Radcliffe is a renowned historian, having published numerous volumes, and is highly respected by learned men everywhere. I have read some of his works myself."

"Her father is *that* Radcliffe?" Lord Charles interposed in surprise. "Why, he is often consulted by some of the Members when they are researching a Question."

"Charles!" Lady Carla exclaimed indignantly, looking at her husband as though he were a traitor. "It is beyond anything that you do not support me. Why, the girl has been on the shelf for years."

"You seem to be remarkably well informed, Carla," Derek remarked with a quizzical expression. "But have you considered that she might have been waiting for a man she could love and truly wish to marry?"

With an incredulous look, Lady Carla declared, "*Never* did I expect to hear *you* of all people mouth such fustian. One could almost imagine you were hipped yourself," she said suspiciously.

The duke burst out laughing. "It is only that I am being

schooled, my dear. You will understand when you speak with Colin."

"Yes, well, I mean to do so as soon as I change from these wet clothes. I hope I do not come down with something from having stood about so long. Where *is* Colin?"

"Changing, also, I imagine. We all came in a little while ago after being caught in the rain ourselves."

"All?" Lady Carla asked keenly. "Who else is here?"

"Julia's sister, Antonia, and Atlee and his daughter Emily. And Aunt Alvinia, of course."

"I wonder *she* did not leave, as she usually does," Lady Carla said caustically. "Isn't—yes, of course. Cecily mentioned that Robert was still dangling after the sister. I *did* meet *her* several years ago. She must be an ape-leader by now."

"I think you would have some argument there, Carla," Derek observed in amusement. "I suspect that most of your information has come from your friend. Considering that a jealous female like Cecily would hardly have kind words for ladies who compete with her, I would have thought that you would not be so gullible as to credit her representations."

With flushed cheeks, feeling uncomfortably intimidated by the duke's abnormally toplofty posture, Lady Carla decided to make her exit and began to walk towards the door.

Derek came quickly forward to grasp her hands, saying teasingly and with a warm smile as he bent to kiss her brow, "Don't be too angry with me, my dear. I apologise for being so ungentlemanly, but I took such strong exception to your bringing Cecily that I forgot my manners. I am truly pleased to see you and am looking forward to hearing all about your travels."

"Oh, well, I daresay I should not have been so presumptuous," Lady Merrill allowed with a pleased expression, for she always responded to words of affection and actually held Derek in third place in her heart. "But surely there will be no problem, since there are so many other guests."

"I hope you may be right," Derek remarked doubtfully. "In

any case, because I do have other obligations, I not propose to dance attendance on the plaguesome countess. She is *your* guest, Carla. You will have to see to her entertainment."

Making a little *moue,* Lady Carla placed her hand on her husband's arm and asked her stepson, with her chin in the air, "Which apartment have you prepared for us?"

"The master suite, my dear. I have not yet taken that over," Derek replied with a wicked grin, amused by her obvious relief that he did not mean to publicise his new strictures.

The door burst open, and Colin came in swiftly to embrace his mother and swing her about. "I must say you took your time about getting here, my lady. I have been impatiently awaiting your appearance." He held her away and looked at her critically. "Well, I do believe I shall have to begin calling you Carla, as Derek does. No one could possibly imagine you old enough to be my mother."

With happiness erasing her sense of ill use, Lady Merrill did appear years younger. She laughed delightedly at Colin's barefaced flattery, accusing him of being a humbug, and showing her great pleasure to see him as she pressed her cheek to his and noted that he was looking in especially high feather.

"Yes, my love, I am in fine fettle and for a very excellent reason. I am anxious for you to meet Julia, Mother. You must love her as I do."

"Oh," Lady Carla said weakly, having for a moment forgotten the delicate point. "Well, we will talk about that after I have changed. I really must get out of these damp clothes. I will send word when I am ready for you to attend me." And with this noncommittal reply, she swept out of the room, leaving her husband to follow after he and Colin had exchanged warm greetings.

Colin stood for a moment looking after them thoughtfully and then turned to Derek with a resigned sigh. "She is not going to take it well, is she?"

"Not from first appearances, it seems," the duke replied sympathetically. "Unfortunately she has allowed Cecily Mervyn to exacerbate her prejudices." Derek proceeded to tell his brother of the conversation that just preceded his entrance. "I'm afraid I was extremely discourteous, Colin. I let my temper get the better of me."

"You *do* have a little problem there once in a while," Colin noted with a grin. "But, my God, Derek! Whatever possessed Mother to bring Cecily with her? It is totally incomprehensible. I am of the mind that she doesn't even like her."

"I know. I haven't quite fathomed that, either. One would have to suppose that she was trying to promote a match, though she did everything she could to prevent what she erroneously imagined might be one of a few years ago when I was so imprudent as to squire Cecily around during a couple of my leaves. I have been trying to depress the lady's aspirations ever since. To find her here in my own house is extremely awkward."

"It seems we are in for an interesting summer," Colin noted facetiously. "I expect I had better alert Julia. I had hoped Mother would be reasonable. It is absolutely absurd that she places such an importance on rank."

"Julia is already aware of her sentiments," Derek told his brother wryly. "She and Tonia were about to come downstairs when our guests arrived and so were treated to a rather theatrical exposition of Carla's prejudices."

"Damn! I meant to be with Julia when she met up with Mother."

"They didn't come down, Colin. I was the only one who knew they were there. And I don't think you need to concern yourself with Julia's reaction. I expect she will be guided by that miserable sister of hers who seemed to find the whole thing exceedingly funny," the duke said darkly.

Colin had to laugh at his brother's rueful expression, and he commented, "I suppose Cecily's demonstrative greeting was remarked as well?"

"Unfortunately, yes."

"I wouldn't worry too much about it," Colin advised. "I don't doubt that the circumstances are well understood."

Derek grinned sheepishly, saying, "Perhaps, but it is a little embarrassing to be caught with a woman hanging on one's neck." Looking at his brother with a twinkling eye, not pretending to misunderstand Colin's innuendo, the duke ventured, "While we are cleverly skirting the issue, I should like to have your opinion of just what Robert's chances are?"

"None at all, according to Julia," Colin replied promptly. "Tonia would never settle for less than a mutual love-match, and she is not so committed, even though he is." Having voiced this encouraging judgement, Colin did not pursue the matter, confident that Derek would follow his reasoning. He asked casually, "Where is Cecily now?"

"In her room, I expect. I told Nestor to prepare a room for her and then left her standing in the hall. I seem to have lost all my gentlemanly instincts. I'm going to visit Aunt Alvinia. You might as well come along. I imagine we will find the Misses Radcliffe in attendance, also."

In this assumption he was correct, for after Julia and Tonia had retreated to their rooms to discuss the implications of the scene they had witnessed, with several irreverent comments by one of them, who meant to make light of the matter to allay her sister's misgivings, they presented themselves to Lady Alvinia and acquainted her with the latest developments.

"Poor Derek," this lady commiserated. "He is going to have his hands full trying to sidestep both Alicia and the countess. He must be furious."

"That was obvious," Tonia agreed with her impish grin. "Cecily was lucky not to find herself on the floor."

Looking at Julia, who seemed unusually pensive, Lady Alvinia reassured her, "Don't tease yourself, my dear. You know Derek is on your side. He will have at least tried to smooth the way."

"I know," Julia acknowledged with a soft smile. "It's just that I am hoping Colin will show restraint. It would make it so much more difficult if there were angry words."

Several more minutes elapsed before the gentlemen joined them, by which time the ladies had exhausted the subject and were ripe for considering additional viewpoints and estimations.

Speaking to his aunt, the duke noted dryly, "I see you have been apprised of our latest disruption."

"Yes, Derek, and I find the Countess of Falmouth's presence highly intriguing."

"By that I hope you don't mean to imply that I have any interest there," the duke said sharply.

"No, no. Do not cut up stiff, my boy," Lady Alvinia admonished. "I just question Carla's purpose."

"You are not alone," her nephew commented irritably.

"Actually," Tonia remarked with a maddening certitude, "it is really quite simple."

Derek looked at her suspiciously as she hesitated, and he demanded, "Well, are you going to share your superior knowledge?"

"It *is* rather a delicate matter," she advised primly, with a suspicious quiver of the lips.

"Which you are *extremely* loathe to discuss," the duke suggested sardonically.

"Not really. I just thought I should warn you," Tonia replied with a grin. "One only has to consider how jealous Colin's mother is of his standing to find the answer—if one has confidential knowledge, that is. You see, early in the year it appeared that Cecily would receive an offer from the Marquess of Janesville. However, the marquess's mother was by no means enamoured of the match, and she began to do a little investigating. Apparently she learned from one of Cecily's sisters-in-law that the late earl, Cecily's husband, had been highly displeased that his wife had not given him an heir. And since he had evidences from a number of other quarters that he could not be at fault, he insisted she see a doctor and had his suspicions confirmed. Needless to say, the marquess backed off when confronted with this information."

"Tonia!" Julia exclaimed in shocked surprise. "Who told you that?"

"Aunt Margot. And you know she is always on top of everything," her sister replied with confidence.

"Well, that does explain it," Lady Alvinia remarked tartly. "Carla is always quick to grasp an advantage for Colin."

"I think it is terribly clever of her myself," Tonia confessed admiringly. "I am quite looking forward to bettering our acquaintance."

Recovering from the force of this unexpectedly revealing information, the gentlemen registered very different reactions. Derek, surprisingly, burst out laughing, not taking the least offense. He shook his head as he said indulgently, "That shameless, wily little schemer. I have to give her credit. I should have guessed what was behind it."

Colin, however, did not take the matter so lightly, feeling an acute embarrassment at the unmasking of this lamentable caprice of his mother, whose excessive ambition for himself he found extremely discomfitting. "This time she has gone beyond what is acceptable," he stated feelingly. "I mean to have it out with her."

Realising Colin was truly outraged and upset, Julia went over to place herself at his side and laid her hand lovingly against his cheek. "Do not take it so seriously, my darling. Try to see the humour of it as the rest of us do. It is really all of a piece, you know. Your mother holds you so dear that she cannot help but want the best for you."

"The best for me would be to give me credit for knowing what I want and to be pleased that I have found it," Colin said stubbornly. "And she knows I have never aspired to being duke. I cannot believe she has become so caught up with the notion herself that she would conceive such a scheme."

"Colin, do try to be calm about it," Tonia admonished, being ready, as always, to accept a challenge. "We were faced with this sort of thing before and came about rather neatly. I propose we use the same strategy."

"I will vouch for its effectiveness," Derek attested with a rueful expression. "Just behave naturally, speak of your engagement as an accomplished fact, and ignore any little vexations cast your way."

They all had to laugh at this evidence of a lesson well learned, and the good-humoured mood spilled over to Colin. He buried his face in Julia's palm and promised, "All right, I will have a go at it. But I will not be pushed too far. And I certainly will not countenance any slight to Julia."

Holding very little hope that there would be none, Tonia did not find the prospects for a subtle victory very promising. She feared that Julia would have a hard time persuading Colin to keep to the plan.

While all these discussions were taking place, the unwelcome guest was very busy in another room of the castle. Derek's unenthusiastic reception rankled Lady Cecily considerably. Consequently, she had spent the better part of an hour venting her ill-humour on her hapless maid, who, being accustomed, and so, inured, to suffering verbal abuse when her mistress was in a temper, had eventually slipped out during a lull to discover whatever tittle-tattle she could about the household. With a strong sense of self-preservation she had learned that her lady could always be beguiled with a report on the backstairs gossip, which usually contained some interesting information that the countess would find useful.

Thus, tuning in a sharp ear, she artfully catechised the servants belowstairs. In a very short time she uncovered at least one confidence that she suspected would intrigue her mistress, being the kind of thing that lent itself to mischief-making. With a sense of obligation she added her own offering (pertaining to the countess's ambitions) to the gossip pool, thinking it only fair, after all, and having found that a little indiscretion generally made for excellent results. Then she returned to her duties, prepared to ingratiate herself with a report on what she had learned. She made mention of Lady Ealand, though she had gained only a faint impression of some irregularity there. But she was able to give a full account of the ill-fated scheme that occasioned the presence of the Earl of Atlee and his daughter at the castle.

The countess received this information with an air of speculation, resolving to keep it in reserve until she found a use for it. She suspected that Lady Carla would much have preferred that match to the one her son had made on his own. Recovering her spirits, she sat at the dressing table to finish her toilette as she revised her strategy for bringing the duke up to scratch. Things had started out badly, and she realized she would have to be more circumspect in her pursuit.

=11=

NESTOR CAME TO Lady Alvinia's chambers to inform Colin that Lady Merrill requested his presence in her boudoir. Anxious to impress his mother with his sincere commitment, the young man rose immediately and kissed Julia lightly. "Wait for me, love. I want us to go downstairs together."

"Colin, my dear, do come in," Lady Carla called gaily when her son appeared at the door. She was dressed in a frilly pink wrapper and was lounging on the elegant rose velvet chaise, presenting a charming picture of supreme luxury. "I feel terribly done up after that dreadful ride today, and I have decided not to join the others for tea. I thought it would be a good time for us to have a private coze. Sit here by me," she invited, patting a place beside her, "and we will talk over our differences."

"What differences, Mother?" Colin asked in feigned surprise. "We have only just come together. How could we be at odds?"

"My dear, surely you know I would not approve of your intention to connect yourself so far beneath your station," Lady Carla admonished, having decided to confront the issue without equivocation, since she felt she already had lost valuable time. "Naturally I hope to convince you to reconsider. Why, with *your* prospects and personal attributes you could look as high as you might."

Colin had to laugh at this highly prejudiced estimation, and he chided her lightly, "Mama, you are certainly labouring under some preposterous misapprehension. From your description one would think I meant to marry the scullery maid. Wherever did you come by such a maggoty notion?"

"Colin, do not try to cozen me," Lady Carla protested indignantly. "You know I said no such thing, but the girl's family

118

has *no* standing at all. What possible advantage can there be in it for you?"

"Excepting the fact that I would be incredibly happy with my lovely wife, you mean?" Colin asked with a challenging glint in his eye.

"Oh, well, as to *that,* my love, I am sure you might find someone more suitable who would please you as well," Lady Carla inferred with a lack of sensitivity that set her son's back up irrevocably. "You did rather rush your fences, Colin. It would have been much more prudent to have looked about for a while. You have only just come home, after all."

"Mama," Colin began, trying to hold himself in check, "I have resolved to keep my temper, but if you persist in making these provoking, derogatory remarks about my chosen bride, whom you have yet to meet, I will not be responsible for my actions. As it happens, though I do not consider it of the least importance, Julia is descended from illustrious lines on both sides of her family, albeit from younger branches. Besides, her aunt, with whom she and Tonia stay in London, is a member in good standing in the *ton.* There is really no reason for you to take such exception to Julia just because her immediate family is not titled."

"If you are speaking of Margot Walton, I do not consider *that* a particular recommendation," Lady Carla commented with a sniff. "She is *shockingly* irregular."

"That's coming it a little strong, Mama," Colin said with a laugh. "She may be a little unusual, but I like her very well."

"Really, Colin, I believe you have taken leave of your senses. I am very much put out with Derek for not exercising more prudence. He should have been with you in London."

"I don't know what difference you think that would have made, Mother. Nothing could have kept me from Julia. I knew her immediately for my very own. And," he added, having reached the limit of his minimal store of patience in this matter, "I find your arguments extremely irrational when, in fact, I am a commoner myself. My children will have no title, you know. Will you hold that against them?"

"Colin!" his mother exclaimed in dismay, "how can you say such a thing?"

"Because it's true," he stated flatly. "I'm sorry to be so plain-spoken, Mama, but I am unhappily come to realize that you have visions of me being a duke one day, an assumption that I find totally abhorrent."

"Well, my dear, you *are* Derek's heir, and several years younger, so it would not be beyond the imagination, after all," Lady Carla said defensively. "Not that I should hope for it—you *know* that I do not. But your son would certainly have prospects."

"You are forgetting a very salient point, Mother," Colin advised. "Derek is still apt to marry and have children himself."

"Do you truly think so?" Lady Carla asked uncertainly, widening her eyes and taking a short breath before conceding, "I suppose he *might,* though he has always seemed so indifferent to the idea. Still," she added, unwittingly compromising herself, "there may not be children. One never can be sure of things like that."

Colin was silent for a moment, sorely disappointed that his mother had, by this seemingly casual remark, confirmed Tonia's presumption. Declining to humour her further, he proceeded to disabuse her of her fantasies. "Mother, at the risk of offending you and seeming disrespectful, I must tell you that your little game is discovered. I hope you will not make yourself look ridiculous by trying to promote a match between Cecily and Derek. Her incapability is known, and I am very much vexed that you would go to such lengths. By your scheming you have placed Derek in an abdominably embarrassing position." Plainly up in arms, he rose and said crossly, "I am too much out of temper to continue this conversation now, so I will leave you to rest. When you come down to dinner, I will introduce you to your future daughter-in-law. I hope you will have come to terms with that and will see fit to treat her with grace." And with this express admonition he turned abruptly and left the room.

Lady Carla stared after him in hurt bewilderment. *Really,* she thought resentfully, whatever has come over Colin—and Derek, too? They both seemed so mettlesome—not like the dear boys they had always been. It was true that the family had not all been together very much these last few years, but surely they could not have changed so much. Perhaps she *had* been a little misguided to have invited Cecily. That is what had set them off, it seemed. Well, she would not pursue the matter. But as for the *other,* she would see about that. She did not mean to back off yet. Colin must come to realise his mistake. Oh, how she wished she and Charles had returned for the Season!

Derek had remained with the ladies a few minutes after Colin left, then decided he should make some effort to perform his duties as host and so went to seek out the earl. Guessing the library to be a most likely choice, he located him promptly. "Am I disturbing you?" he asked as he entered to find his two guests engrossed in their reading, Emily with a tale by Maria Edgeworth, a favourite of Lady Alvinia, and her father with the latest edition of *The Quarterly Review.*

They both looked up, and the earl asked curiously, "Have you resolved all your problems?"

"Being a little optimistic, aren't you?" the duke retorted dryly. Smiling at Emily, he said, "If you would like to join the ladies, Emily, they are with Aunt Alvinia in her sitting room."

"Oh, well, I did not want to impose," she replied hesitantly.

"You would be welcome, I'm sure," the duke told her. "They are just relaxing."

"Well, then, perhaps I will, your grace," the girl accepted happily and rose immediately to leave the gentlemen in private.

"I assume from your lack of cheer that Lady Merrill means to create difficulties," the earl noted with raised brows.

"Yes, but were it only that, it would be an easy matter since the rest of us are in accord. The aggravation is that Carla had the unwarrantable presumption to invite Cecily Mervyn," Derek expounded angrily.

"*Cecily* is here?" Robert exclaimed incredulously. "Good Lord!"

Derek then acquainted his friend with the main points of his recent conversations. "At least this ill-conceived trick convinced me that it was time to assert myself," he declared firmly.

Nestor came then to announce that the ladies were entertaining in the drawing room and would be pleased to receive the gentlemen.

Derek laughed and remarked, "That sounds like one of Aunt Alvinia's thinly disguised commands. Shall we accept?"

"Naturally," the earl replied promptly, having become impatient for Tonia to reappear.

When they had all settled themselves comfortably before a pleasant fire that warded off the chill of the bleak day, Derek asked Colin, "How did it go?"

With a wry face, the younger man replied, "Not very well, but I left before I managed to sink myself beyond reproach." Before he could explain further, Lord Charles entered with Cecily, who had charged her maid to keep a sharp eye out for one of her travelling companions so that she would not have to make a solo appearance.

In resignation, the duke presented her to Lady Alvinia and to Emily and then said, "I believe you know everyone else."

"Oh, yes," she acknowledged with a bright smile all around. "How are you, Robert? We missed you this Season. And Colin— Antonia—Julia. How nice to see you. I had no idea there would be such a gathering here. It is quite delightful."

Knowing this assertion did not echo the lady's true sentiments, Tonia could not resist throwing a little barb. "And so it has been, Cecily. Glenview is spectacularly beautiful, and the duke has been a most gracious host."

Derek suppressed a smile as the countess looked at her

sharply, trying to decide if she were going to face unexpected competition from that quarter. Surely Robert's presence would preclude that vexation?

After an hour or so of vapid conversation, as the easy familiarity practised by the household before this latest invasion seemed to be in abeyance now that an incompatible personality had entered the scene, the ladies and gentlemen dispersed to dress for the evening.

Lady Carla and Lord Charles were the last to enter the drawing room, where the others had gathered to wait for dinner to be announced. Colin stepped forward immediately taking the countess's arm to guide her to where Julia stood, flanked by Derek and Tonia.

"Mother, it is my great happiness to introduce you to Miss Julia Radcliffe, my chosen bride," Colin announced with a quaint formality.

Julia smiled sweetly and curtsied. "How do you do, Lady Merrill? I am very pleased to make your acquaintance."

With reluctance Lady Carla fairly acknowledged to herself that the girl was uncommonly lovely and showed herself prettily mannered, besides. But, determined not to be swayed by outward appearances, she merely nodded somewhat stiffly and said, "I believe I have seen you in town, though perhaps it may have been several years ago."

"Very likely, my lady," Julia responded amiably. "My sister and I always go to London for the Season. You have met Antonia?"

"Quite possibly," Lady Carla conceded, turning her head to look at the small lady standing beside Julia, and feeling a twinge of surprise to discover that, contrary to her expectation that the elder Miss Radcliffe would appear an ape-leader, she was not only very well preserved but positively youthful.

Tonia bowed politely. "We *have* met, though it was some time ago. I daresay you will not remember. It was at an assembly at Lady Cartland's—a dreadful crush, I recall. I remember you wore the loveliest blue gown I had ever seen, and I *so* wished I had anything half so elegant. Not that I could have worn blue, of course. It does not become me at all. But it suits *you* wonderfully."

"Do you think so, my dear?" Lady Merrill queried with a pleased smile, succumbing easily to this barefaced cajolery. "I do recollect the occasion, now that you have reminded me, though I *cannot* picture the gown."

"Can you not? Well, no doubt it was one of many and of no special import to you," Tonia said smoothly and then directed her attention elsewhere. "Emily, my dear," she said encouragingly, "do come present yourself to Lady Merrill."

The young girl stepped forward and curtsied, saying diffidently, "I am pleased to meet you, my lady."

"Why, Robert," Lady Merrill exclaimed in astonishment, "where have you been keeping this pretty child? I didn't realise she was such a young lady."

"Yes, Carla. Emily has grown up and has left the Academy. We have had happy times, these past few weeks, becoming better acquainted."

"I'm sure you must have," Lady Carla allowed with an approving nod. Her eyes travelled to the elderly lady sitting on the couch, and she said brusquely, "Hello, Alvinia. I trust you are feeling well?"

"Why yes, Carla, I am, as a matter of fact," Lady Alvinia responded warily.

"Well, I am glad to hear it. I though you might be ailing, since you did not make one of your excursions," Lady Merrill remarked suggestively.

"Naturally it *did* occur to me to do so," Lady Alvinia replied in kind. "But when Colin was so accommodating as to bring two such charming, exceptional girls to entertain me, I could not possibly think of leaving."

The duke had moved next to Tonia, and she, looking at him, her eyes brimming with laughter, said softly, "Oh, dear."

"You should talk, you shameless imp. I am persuaded your little discourse was a complete fabrication. It would have served you right if she *had* remembered her gown."

"It likely *was* blue, which is obviously her favourite colour," Tonia murmured defensively as she gazed upon Lady Merrill's toilette—a blue gown, blue slippers, sapphires around her neck and arms and a blue feather in her coiffure.

Derek just shook his head and then, acknowledging Nestor's signal, moved to offer his arm to his stepmother to lead the procession to the dining room.

Dinner that evening was a merry affair. All expressed genuine interest in hearing stories of the many adventures and pleasures that the travellers had experienced in their year abroad. The party remained long at table, so that the gentlemen dallied only a short time over their port before rejoining the ladies in the drawing room where the main subject for discussion was the ball at Ealand Hall two nights hence.

"I must say it was impulsive of Alicia to schedule it so soon when it was not known when we would arrive," Lady Carla demurred, a little piqued.

"She *was* concerned about that, Lady Merrill," Julia reassured her. "But Colin persuaded the baroness that you must be here this week so she went ahead with her plans."

"Well," Lady Carla said, somewhat mollified, "I'm sure it is very amiable of her to hold a ball to welcome us. Later, we must plan an entertainment of our own. It will be expected, of course."

Colin spoke up quickly before his mother could get too caught up in her inventions. "Derek has already promised our neighbours that he would stage a grand ball this summer, Mother."

"Oh," Lady Carla said weakly, a little discomfitted at being faced with this subtle reminder that she no longer could play first fiddle here.

"We will wait a little while, Carla," Derek suggested affably. And then in an attempt to soothe her ruffled feathers, he requested, "But when we are ready, I would appreciate it if you would take charge."

With a pleased expression—her stepson was showing himself to be a dear boy, after all—Lady Merrill readily consented, "Well, of course, Derek, I would be happy to. But you must give me a little advance notice."

"Yes, Carla, I will do that," he promised with a gentle smile. And on this happy resolution, the party broke up for the night.

The next morning, when the early risers were enjoying a leisurely breakfast, relieved of the presence of two disquieting ladies who were not yet accustomed to country hours, Lady Alicia, who had a penchant for early visits, arrived to confirm the rumours of the new arrivals and to ascertain the identity of the third guest.

"Cecily Mervyn" meant nothing to the baroness, but when Tonia further identified her as the Countess of Falmouth, she immediately knew her for the lady whose name had been linked with Derek's several years before, and she felt an instant antagonism. Declining to wait until the rest of the household appeared, she spoke to Tonia. "If you are still available, I would welcome your assistance. So many things are piling up, and John suggested I call on you to inspect the gardens and order the flower arrangements. There is not a great deal to choose from at the moment, I'm afraid."

"You may supplement from our gardens, if you wish," Derek offered.

"Thank you, Derek. I will leave that to Tonia, if she is agreeable."

"Yes, Alicia, I should enjoy making myself useful. I will be ready in a few minutes," Tonia replied, happy to have another excuse to avoid Robert, who was becoming extremely vexed that there never seemed to be any opportunity to claim her exclusive company.

Alicia had come in her smart little carriage, and soon the two ladies set off at a spanking pace.

"What is Lady Falmouth doing here?" the baroness asked bluntly.

"Trying to raise her station, of course," Tonia responded.

"What does she look like? How old is she?"

"She's a rather flamboyant blonde, about twenty-seven, I'd judge."

A flick of Alicia's whip sent the horses surging forward, forcing Tonia to hold on tightly to keep her seat.

"Alicia," she said caustically, "since I value my life, I will tell you that Derek did not invite her and is very angry with Lady Carla for having brought her."

The baroness slowed the pace and glanced at Tonia with a satisfied smile.

"Alicia," Tonia ventured resolutely, "I know that I am shockingly out of line to concern myself with your private affairs, but the fact is that I like you and John very well, and I hate to see you jeopardising your standing with him, particularly when I am persuaded that you are actually very much attached to each other."

"Really, Antonia, you presume too much," the baroness snapped irritably.

"Just how much do you expect your husband to overlook?" Tonia persevered, undaunted.

"John has always been aware of my feelings for Derek, and he married me anyway," Alicia revealed almost resentfully.

"Well, I see you mean to persist in this folly," Tonia said in disgust. "I leave you to your just deserts. No doubt you and the countess will treat the company to a deplorable spectacle."

"You said Derek was not interested in her," Alicia commented smugly.

"His lack of interest hasn't fazed *you,*" Tonia retorted trenchantly, feeling uncommonly contentious. "Why do you expect it will dampen her?"

They were met by the baron at the hall. As he helped them both out of the carriage, Alicia requested uncivilly, "Perhaps you will direct Antonia to the gardens, John. I have other things to do." She walked away abruptly.

The baron looked at Tonia inquisitively. "We had words on the way over," she admitted ruefully.

"Do not be concerned, Antonia. Alicia rarely holds a grudge," the baron reassured her. And, being pleased to have an excuse to remain in her company, he offered his arm and led her to the walled garden.

At the castle, Lady Carla and Lady Cecily found themselves breakfasting alone at eleven o'clock, since all other members of the household had gone off to follow their various pursuits. Derek and both earls had ridden off to make the rounds, as Lord Charles was interested to inspect the improvements that were in progress. Colin remained behind, unwilling to leave Julia at his mother's mercy. With Emily, they could be seen across the lawn engaging in target practice at the archery field.

Displeased with the prospect of having to find her own amusements, Lady Falmouth resentfully decided to throw a cat among the pigeons. "It is too bad Derek did not follow through in his designs, isn't it?" she remarked cryptically.

Lady Merrill raised her eyebrows at this and asked, "Whatever do you mean?"

"Oh, I thought you would have heard as I did," Lady Cecily said in surprise. And she proceeded to reveal the proposed match between Colin and Emily.

"I *knew* Derek would have ordered plans for Colin's future!" Lady Carla cried triumphantly. "But why did he not make a push?" she pondered in vexation. "Perhaps it is still in the wind. I will certainly speak to him about it." And with visions of having her hopes fulfilled, after all, she reconciled herself to entertaining Cecily and escorted her on a tour of the castle and the gardens.

That evening Lady Carla unaccountably began to shower Emily with attention, making a particular point of commending her for being a dutiful daughter. "It is always gratifying to meet a young girl who is willing to follow her father's advice in matters that concern her future."

"Oh, yes," Emily agreed ingenuously. "And Papa is *so* understanding. He has promised that I shall have a Season next year, and Tonia is going to sponsor me."

Taken aback by this unwelcome revelation, Lady Carla protested, reaching out to pat the girl's hand, "Now my dear,

128

surely you will not disappoint me. I had my heart on bringing you out myself."

"Oh," Emily said uncertainly, looking across at Tonia for help. She really was confounded by this precipitate offer, unable to imagine why Lady Carla should express such interest in her. "That is extremely kind of you, Lady Merrill, but Tonia and I have already been making plans."

Warding off further importunities by the determined lady, and hoping to save his daughter some embarrassment, Lord Atlee interposed, "It is quite settled, Carla. I have approved the scheme."

"Oh, well, of course, I see," Lady Merrill said, backing off reluctantly, recognizing that Robert was telling her that he preferred present arrangements.

Later in the drawing room, however, she continued to indulge her fancy. Taking exception to her son's obvious contentment as he sat next to Julia, holding her hand, she called to him with a little pout, "Colin, do come sit here by me. We have had so little chance to talk."

"I'm afraid My Lady has gotten wind of our regrettable *faux pas,*" Derek murmured to Robert.

"So it seems," the earl agreed ruefully. "Remarkably tenacious female, ain't she?"

The day of the ball was comparatively free of tensions. Most of the day, for the ladies at least, was devoted to preparing their toilettes, which included the time-consuming task of washing, drying, and curling their hair. Emily, caught up in the excitement of going to her very first ball, flitted back and forth incessantly between her own and the Radcliffes' chambers, learning what they were going to wear and how they were going to dress their hair (never a concern of Tonia's), taking part in choosing appropriate accessories and asking for opinions and approval on her own appearance.

Finally, at half-past six, a gay caravan of three carriages headed for the Ealand estate, where the Gleniew party had been invited to partake of a dinner before the other guests arrived.

Tonia saw at once that the baron's estimation of Alicia's efficiency was confirmed. Everything was in perfect order; the servants performed their duties with alacrity and finesse; and the menu, consisting of a clear broth, smoked mackerel, glazed ham, crouton potatoes and a choice of vegetables, with fruit and cheeses offered for dessert, was excellently prepared and considerately delicate, a heavy meal being undesirable before an evening of dancing. In all the rooms, the profusion of roses, which Tonia had ordered, along with ferns and other greenery, gave off a pleasant aroma that was wafted throughout the house by a gentle breeze blowing in at the open windows, the day being fortuitously pleasant.

During dinner, as could have been expected, Alicia and Cecily developed a hearty dislike of one another, quickly becoming aware of their rivalry. The dislike deepened in the course of the evening, fed by the circumstance that the duke held himself aloof from both, and danced with each of them but once.

On his part, the duke, after a time, could not fail to notice the baron's discreet but obvious partiality for Tonia's company. So he made it a point to establish himself in their presence whenever possible, not wanting to set tongues awagging.

When the dancing began, Tonia was always partnered and could be seen swirling abandonedly about the room. When he claimed her for their second waltz, Derek said, "If you are always in such demand, it is no wonder you have little credit with certain other females."

She grinned impishly, making him want to kiss her on the spot, as she retorted, "*Certain* females can better take themselves to account."

Emily contented herself with participating in the few country dances Alicia had ordered and did not feel herself too put upon, as there were three other young girls who faced the same strictures. Their little group held court in one corner, attended by several of the younger men, who occasionally deserted them to dance with the older females, flaunting their more liberated status. But they generally returned to the fold, being impressed with the presence of an earl's charming and eligible daughter.

Lady Carla, always susceptible to being cajoled by amiable company, was occupied with her erstwhile neighbours, who were eager to be entertained with an account of her travels, so that her attention was diverted from Colin and Julia, who danced with each other almost exclusively under the indulgent eyes of the other guests, all of whom judged them a remarkably handsome couple.

The evening proved a tremendous success. And if the hostess and one other lady were less than satisfied with their progress in a certain matter, no one else had cause for complaint. Lady Alvinia pleasurably spent the hours in animated conversation with Reverend Dodson and other elderly guests. And Lord Atlee congratulated himself that he had managed to claim three dances with Tonia, a *coup* ill-humouredly recorded by another gentleman who was hampered from claiming his own advantage by several plaguesome restraints.

=12=

EXCEPT FOR LADY Alvinia, Lady Cecily and Lord and Lady Merrill, the other members of the household rose at a reasonable hour that Sunday morning and drove off to Southwell to attend church. When they returned to the castle, the tardy risers had just made their appearance.

Everyone voiced approval of the baroness's outstanding success, and several notes were dispatched to express appreciation for so admirable an entertainment. Emily was especially vociferous, declaring herself excessively pleased to have made several new friends, both ladies *and* gentlemen, who had invited her to join them in some of their amusements while she remained at Glenview.

Regretting that she had been distracted from her purpose by last evening's socializing, Lady Carla determined to pursue the matter more resolutely. Contriving to isolate Emily so that she could sound the girl out and identify herself as an ally, she linked arms with her familiarly, as they all strolled out onto the terrace, and coaxed, "Come, my dear, do walk with me in the gardens. I should like for us to become better acquainted."

Casting a quick look at Tonia, Emily was a little disconcerted to receive a wink from that lady. But she accepted Lady Carla's invitation graciously and allowed herself to be led to a little arbour at the edge of the formal garden.

They sat on a small stone bench and Lady Carla sighed happily. "Oh, how pleasant it is to be here in the summer. Glenview is *so* lovely. I have always been particularly fond of it. I came here as a young bride, you know—about your age. I was terrified at first," she confessed intimately. "I know, you see, how unfortunate it is not to have a mother to talk to if you are a young girl, confused by an affair of the heart. I hope you will look upon me as a substitute

132

and feel free to confide in me if you find yourself in some sort of quandary."

"Why, thank you, Lady Carla," Emily said politely, thinking she never seemed able to quite fathom this lady's conversation, and wondering if she were just the least bit scatterbrained.

"I thought perhaps you might have suffered a disappointment recently," Lady Carla hinted, moving inexorably to the point.

"Do you mean about Colin?" Emily asked candidly with a little giggle. "Oh, no! *That* was over before it was ever begun. Unbeknownst to my father and the duke, he and Julia were already bespoke."

"But, my dear, it is such a very recent thing and not final yet, so you must not give up hope," Lady Carla said confidentially.

Emily looked at the older lady in bewilderment and stammered, "I—I do not understand what you mean, Lady Merrill. Julia and Colin plan to be married in September."

"So soon?!" Lady Carla exclaimed with a little start. "I had not been told. But Emily, are you not attracted to Colin?" she prompted single-mindedly.

"Oh, I think he is a *splendid* gentleman. Julia is very lucky," the girl responded artlessly, persuading her companion to take heart until she added, "but so is he. I *adore* Julia. She is the sweetest, most amiable girl I have ever met."

"Well, I do think it must have been terribly distressing that Sayer and the earl had raised your hopes and then did *nothing* to insure that they were realized," Lady Carla pursued unswervingly.

"But Lady Carla," Emily protested, finally coming to understand what lay behind this *tête-à-tête*, "I would never want to be married to a man who loved someone else. How dreadful it would be! I am *so* glad that I have met Julia and Tonia, for I have come to realise that it is not at all necessary to marry just anyone. I have decided to follow their example and wait until I find my true love."

Feeling a maddening sense of frustration that this foolish girl's head was so filled with romantic notions that she would not see the advantage of connecting herself with the only brother of the unmarried Duke of Sayer, Lady Carla gave up on this tack in exasperation and abruptly suggested they return to join the others.

Immediately they reached the terrace, she approached her stepson. "Derek, may I speak privately with you?"

"Of course, my dear. Shall we go into my study?" he suggested affably as he held out his arm.

When they had disappeared, Emily took Tonia's hand and pulled her aside. "Tonia, I'd like to talk to you."

"I thought you might," her mentor murmured as she walked with her down the terraced steps.

Emily stopped and stared. "You know what that was all about? Is that why you winked at me?"

With a prim expression, Tonia protested, "I'm sure I did no such thing!"

"Yes, you did! But *how* did you *know*?"

"It has become very very apparent that the countess fancies you as a daughter-in-law, my love."

"I don't understand. It is a settled thing between Colin and Julia."

"Lady Carla has not yet accepted that. You see, Emily, it is not only females who must suffer the ambitious designs of their families."

"Oh. Well, I was not at all perceptive, at least not at first. I daresay Lady Merrill thinks me the greatest ninnyhammer."

"Very likely. But that does not seem to have deterred her from her purpose," Tonia commented dryly, provoking the indignant young lady to giggle and accuse, "Tonia, you are a perfectly wretched lady!"

In the duke's study, the countess assumed an air of outrage. "Derek, *why* did you not tell me of the agreement between you and Robert regarding a match between Colin and Emily?" she demanded.

"Because, Carla, it was entirely irrelevant," her stepson

replied. "And since that regrettable scheme will always haunt me, reminding me of one of the most reprehensible performances of my life, I have had no desire to publish it."

"Really, Derek, you are speaking in riddles. I wish you will tell me just what happened."

"I was thoroughly set down for my presumptions," he said briefly. "What it amounts to, my dear, is that it was brought home to me in no uncertain terms that Colin is a much wiser man than I am. He knows what he wants and has sufficient self-esteem and self-confidence to speak his piece and stand firm in his convictions. I cannot be too critical of your impression that the ordering of his life is our business since I unhappily presumed in that area myself. But, Carla, Colin really *is* his own man now. These years, when he served his country honourably and well, he grew in stature on his own and need look up to no one. I wonder if you realise how highly regarded he was by his men and his superiors. He has become an exceptional man, and we did not do him enough honour."

Much awed by this extravagant encomium of her beloved son, Lady Merrill sat silently for a moment. But then her single-minded concern prompted her to make yet another exertion. "I'm sure I am very gratified to hear you speak so laudably of Colin, Derek. But it does not explain why you did not try at least to influence him."

"I did, Carla, which is the part that does me little credit. However, Colin would not be bullied, and I soon realized that I was in danger of irreparably damaging my intimate relationship with the one person I value above all others. So I quickly came to terms with Colin's decision, which I subsequently have approved wholeheartedly. He and Julia are exceptionally well matched. It will be a very happy marriage."

"But Emily is such a charming girl. And besides, as an only child she would have a large portion—" Lady Merrill began desperately.

"There is no profit continuing in this vein," Derek interrupted, tiring of her arguments. "Robert and I have scotched all thought of the match, and Emily herself does not wish for it. Most important of all, Colin is firmly and happily committed to marrying Julia Radcliffe. Tell me, Carla, considering that the engagement has been announced, would you really wish that Colin cry off? Think how he would appear in the eyes of society. It just isn't done, you know."

"Well, of course, I did not mean for *him* to do so. But I thought *she* could be persuaded in some way."

"If you are making the unworthy suggestion that we should buy her off, I will tell you that you had best order your thoughts before you alienate Colin irrevocably. Don't you realise that you are skating on thin ice now?" Derek said, in exasperation. "He would have broken with you immediately over this if Julia hadn't persuaded him to give you time to get used to the idea. And as for Julia's dowry, perhaps Colin neglected to tell you that she is endowed with some five thousand pounds a year, a legacy from one of her great-aunts. It is not inconsiderable."

"Oh!—oh, no. It is a handsome sum," Lady Carla said in surprise. "I had no idea. Who was the aunt?"

"There were two of them," Derek told her, resigning himself to gratifying her pretensions. "Daughters of a marquess whose title has died out."

"Well!—I *do* think I might have been advised of such pertinent matters," she complained indignantly.

"And so you might have been, my dear, if you had not rushed your fences," the duke said gently, observing that she seemed suspiciously near to tears.

Lady Merrill was now as repentant as it was her nature to be, and Derek went to sit beside her, to take her hands in his and seek to bring her around completely with a full revelation. "I will tell you the rest of it now so you will not be worried about Colin's position and his prospects," he said, and he proceeded to disclose the distribution of property and funds he had ordered so that his brother would be excellently established as a wealthy landowner in his own right.

"Derek!" Lady Carla cried in joyful astonishment. "That is

wonderfully generous of you. I did not imagine you would be so largehearted. Both estates are quite extensive, and—oh, my dear boy," she almost sobbed, wiping away tears before throwing her arms around him. "I am so pleased! And you may be sure I will not tease Colin further about—the other."

There was a warning knock before the door opened. "Come in, Charles." Derek invited. "If you have been worried that we would come to cuffs, you can see you are off the mark."

With a watery smile, Lady Carla tapped him on the arm and chided playfully, "Derek, what a humbug you are." She took her husband by the hand to tell him in jubilant accents how happily everything had been resolved.

With a grateful look at Derek, which silently thanked him for having clarified the situation and having provided for Colin so magnanimously, Lord Charles put his arm around his wife, saying, "I am pleased that you have come to accept Colin's right to choose his bride, my dear. I could not support your designs, for I would not want to deny any man the happiness of marrying a lady he loves, being so pleasantly established myself."

"Charles!" Lady Carla cried with charmingly pink cheeks, "what a lovely thing to say. And *why* did you not put it like that to me before?" she pouted, already having dismissed from her mind her unreasonable preconceived notions.

"It was remiss of me not to, my love," her husband replied soothingly, with a conspiratorial smile at the duke.

A little while later, after Lady Carla had repaired the damage done to her toilette by her emotional outburst, the whole company gathered in the drawing room for tea. It soon became apparent that Lady Merrill had reconciled herself to the match, as she conspicuously turned a benevolent eye on the happy couple. She addressed several remarks to them, signalling her change of heart, and was so impressed by Julia's charming manner and obviously forbearing nature that she was disposed to think Derek was very likely right in his estimation of the girl's sterling character.

Tonia watched this speedy evolution with interest. Moving

casually to where the duke stood with Atlee, she asked teasingly, "Did you wave a magic wand?"

"No," Derek said with a grin. "Did you have one I might have borrowed? It would have been much easier."

Tonia laughed and said, "Well, success speaks, whatever the method. I congratulate you."

Derek bowed in acknowledgment, and with a glint in his eye advised, "I had so many problems to resolve that I decided I had better get on with it," being highly amused by Tonia's deliberately incurious acceptance of his cryptic remark.

During these last several days, Lady Cecily found herself very much on the fringe of the group's amusements. Often she did try to initiate a conversation, but since all her offerings concerned the vagaries of the *ton,* a subject of only cursory interest to most of the others who were glad for a respite from the conceits of polite society, she was reduced to holding court with Lady Carla, who, having been away for almost twleve months, was eager to catch up on all the latest gossip in this year which had seen the departure of several notables, or with Emily, who learned a good deal more than was proper for her tender years.

The next few days passed pleasantly, as a variety of diversions provided entertainment for everyone. Most plans were conceived spontaneously, as the capricious weather was always a deciding factor in any consideration of outdoor activities.

Tonia contrived to spend some time at her painting, but not as much as she would have liked, and she was fast approaching a state of rebellion, finding herself always in company, with Robert at her side. She had become jealous of her time in the summer months, when she concentrated her efforts on her art, and this never-ending socializing was putting her out of temper.

The Countess of Falmouth soon learned that her late arrival on the scene each morning often denied her any part in the others' activities. They seemed to be a remarkably energetic group, regrettably inclined to behave like a pack of rustics, generally rising at an unseemly hour. Finally concluding that she could not hope to land the duke if she rarely ever saw him, she began to come down early in the morning and insinuate herself into one or the other group, placing herself in Derek's company whenever possible.

To thwart this manoeuvring, the duke took to arranging that he, Tonia, Robert and Emily usually make up a foursome, not only during the day but also in the evening when sides or partners were chosen for parlour games. In this way, hoping to get himself out of one hobble, he was fair in the way of getting into another. Emily, finding all this marked attention from so eminent, charming and attractive a gentleman extremely flattering, could be excused for misinterpreting his motives and, for that matter, her own response.

Lady Alvinia congratulated herself for not succumbing to her usual temptation to leave when the countess was in residence, discovering that she and Carla could actually carry on an amiable conversation. They both had come to acknowledge the fact that there was no longer any cause for rivalry between them in the matter of being first oars in the castle. Lady Carla, with surprising equanimity, had accepted her stepson's new position. And Lady Alvinia without resentment visualised the end of her reign, understanding that Derek had a new candidate in mind, a prospect that she welcomed and approved without equivocation.

Lord and Lady Merrill spent some time visiting friends in the neighbourhood and often joined Julia and Colin in pleasant coversation, for Lady Carla had become unabashedly quite taken with her future daughter-in-law, whom she judged a lovely girl. She confided to her husband that this was only as it must be, after all, since Colin could never have chosen an other than superior bride.

Alicia and Lord John were also frequent visitors and hosts, a circumstance that suited Tonia admirably, since the baron usually sought her out, allowing her not only to forward her purpose but also to avoid being too available to her persistent suitor.

Finally Tonia decided to desert the company, and announced her intention to spend a part of every day at her work, letting it be known that she did not want to be distracted by an attendant, an appeal that was understood and respected, if not welcomed, by all. So each fine afternoon she gathered her materials and commissioned Tom to transport her to the lake, where she worked diligently on her canvas, which quickly began to emerge as one of her better paintings.

On these afternoons the duke usually managed to occupy himself with estate affairs, sometimes accompanied by the earl. He was becoming extremely impatient to pursue a particular matter, and he inhospitably tried to imagine some way he could rid himself of the inhibiting presence of several dispensable guests. Unfortunately, none of them seemed to have the faintest intention of quitting the scene on his or her initiative.

One day, coming back early from his rounds and finding everyone gone except for Lady Alvinia, Julia, and Colin, who had declined to accompany the others on an excursion to Edwinstow, Derek decided to take advantage of the moment. "Where *has* Tonia been hiding out?" he asked purposefully.

Julia and Colin looked at each other significantly and then informed him that she was down by the lake near the temple. With a satisfied grin, Derek went to command a horse from the stable and rode off to invade the artist's privacy.

When Tonia heard his approach, she looked up momentarily and then returned to work on the canvas, not exhibiting the least surprise to see him as he dismounted and came to stand beside her—almost, in fact, seeming to have expected him.

He looked at her work critically. "I see you have been making excellent progress," he commented favourably. "It is extremely good."

"Do you think so?" she asked as she leaned back and studied it herself. "I am glad to hear you say so. I had been rather impressed with it myself, but could not quite trust my judgement, since I am naturally prejudiced."

Derek laughed and declared, "I claim the option to buy it if you should chose to sell."

"If it turns out really well, I will give it to you," Tonia promised.

"I accept, and I will hold you to it," he responded promptly. He stood watching a while longer, though it could not be said that he found the canvas the main attraction. It was not often that he could indulge his fancy to look at Tonia with unguarded eyes. He loved this girl, he knew, and he wished nothing more than to spend his life with her in just such an intimate setting. He realised that she was attracted to him but, given what he had heard of her skittishness, he was not yet sure enough to put it to the touch. Besides, there were obstacles to be overcome— Robert, most importantly. As he stood there contemplating these interesting speculations, he became fascinated by a loose tendril that curled just at the curve of her neck and shoulders. Finding it irresistible, he leaned impulsively over to brush his lips over the spot.

"Derek!" Tonia exclaimed, starting indignantly. "Just *what* do you think you are about? How *dare* you take such a liberty? As you mean to behave improperly, I will thank you to leave immediately. If you are in *that* kind of mood, there are other ladies conveniently nearby who would welcome your attentions."

Derek had to laugh at these protestations, speculating that if he were so imprudent as to follow her recommendations, she might be quick to ring a peal over him.

Pretending to take umbrage, Tonia turned from his teasing eyes in a huff and proceeded to ignore him, a move that did not have the effect of depressing the duke. He was determined to make her understand that he had serious aspirations.

"It is rather warm today—do you mind if I remove my coat?" he asked with an easy familiarity.

"No," she replied absently, her eyes on her painting.

He did so and folded it carefully to put under his head as he stretched lazily on the ground. With a contented sigh, he said musingly, "Tonia, I should very much like to meet your mother and father. Do you think they could be persuaded to join us here?"

"Very likely," Tonia told him forthrightly. "Colin has seduced Father with a recital of your accomplishments, you know. I do not think he would need much persuading."

Derek laughed and promised he would see to it. He did not disturb her further, feeling lulled by the peace of the setting and his pleasure in just being with her away from the bustle of the castle, which at the moment housed far more people than he would have wished.

Some time later Tonia heard a faint rumble. After remarking the unclouded sky, she turned to look at the duke and almost laughed aloud. "Why, that miserable man is actually asleep," she thought. A smile spread over her face as she studied him lying there, completely relaxed, looking younger than his years. He really was a handsome man, with his strong, clean-cut features and his thick chestnut-coloured hair, cut in the untidy Brutus fashion and showing just a little grey at the sides. She had an absurd impulse to take a liberty herself and run her hands through it. He kept himself in good physical condition with his daily riding and walking about his estate, and he had a healthy, tanned complexion that contrasted strikingly with the stark whiteness of his shirt. As she gazed at him a strange awareness seemed to envelop her, and she felt unnaturally light-headed. She had an impression of having walked a long way in the dark and of at last seeing a light at the end of a tunnel. What on earth was the matter with her? She hoped she was not coming down with something.

It was not remarkable, considering that she had come to believe herself immune, that she did not recognise the debilitating symptoms that often accompany the emergence of true love. And, in spite of her usually quick perception, it was some moments before she even reached the point of suspecting that she had unwittingly become one of Cupid's victims. But when that possibility did occur to her, she very soon acknowledged the truth of it. At the same time it came to her without a doubt that

Derek had found himself in the same hobble. A happy glow came over her as she realised that she actually *was* recording Glenview for posterity and that the posterity would be hers. With this thought to gratify her, she sighed deeply and applied herself with renewed interest to her painting.

Derek stirred a few minutes later, and as it was getting late in the afternoon, she decided she had better waken him. "Derek," she called softly. "Derek—"

He sat up with a start. "Good Lord! Have I actually been asleep?"

"It sounded like it," she teased him.

He laughed. "You, my girl, are absolutely incorrigible. A proper lady would never mention my ungentlemanly lapse. Tom will come for you soon, and I suppose I should go back first for appearances's sake. Help me with my coat, will you Tonia?"

With a shake of her head, she rose to accommodate him. "Really, Derek, it is beyond me why men must be moulded into their coats so that they cannot dress themselves."

By now they could hear a cart approaching so Derek quickly buttoned his coat, mounted his horse and rode off in another direction as he said with a wicked grin "'Til next time," prompting Tonia to smile smugly at his departing back.

═══13═══

THE BARON AND baroness were expected for dinner that evening, and Tonia had to scramble to get ready, as she had to spend more than the usual time removing the paint from her hands and from several stray places on her arms and face. Finally, having made herself presentable, she hurried down to the drawing room, where everyone was already gathered waiting for her to appear before they should go into dinner.

"I am so sorry," she apologised breathlessly, "but I did not think you would have me come down covered with speckles. I was especially slipshod today, and it took me longer than usual to remove the paint."

"Really, Antonia," Lady Cecily said condescendingly, "I did not know you took yourself so seriously as an artist. It is quite amusing."

"Yes, yes it is," Tonia agreed, seeming to misunderstand her meaning. "I enjoy my work tremendously"—a flat assertion that effectively silenced her would-be detractor.

During dinner, the baron said, "Antonia, we made an agreement earlier, if you will remember. I would show you my Turner, and you would let me see some of your canvases."

"So we did, John," Tonia acknowledged with her dimpled smile, "but they do not just appear out of the blue, you know, and I have had very little time to work. However, these past few days I did apply myself to one I had started soon after I arrived here, and it is very nearly finished. I mean to put it aside for a week or so and then look at it again to decide what must be done. If you would like to see what I have accomplished so far, I will show it to you after dinner."

"Yes, Antonia, I should indeed," said Lord John.

Later, in the drawing room, an easel was set up, and Tonia brought out her painting for display. Everyone gathered around, from either curiosity or interest, and while some, who regarded works of art as mere wall coverings, were not greatly impressed, others, more knowledgeable, recognized the composition as a work of considerable merit.

The baron confirmed his standing as a dilettante by conversing competently with Tonia on mechanics, perspective, colours, light and other artistic aspects. "I would very much like to add this to my collection, Antonia," he said. "I hope you will be agreeable to selling it to me."

Tonia was about to protest that she had rather decided she might like to keep it herself, but was forestalled when the duke intervened. "Hold on there, John. It is already promised. I happened upon Tonia painting today, and when I made a bid for it, she magnanimously offered to give it to me."

Tonia laughed. "That's right, John," she allowed. "And it is, after all, a scene of Glenview."

"Well," the baron said reasonably, "if that is to be the criterion for first choice, then we shall have to invite you to the hall to depict one of our views. What do you think, Alicia? Shall we commission Antonia to paint for us?"

"If you wish," the baroness agreed affably. "I'm sure you are a better judge of what is good than I am, though I must say that I do like this painting very much. And it would be nice to have something particular done—the old stone-walled garden perhaps."

"There! We are agreed, Antonia. When can you start?" Lord John asked eagerly.

"Well," Tonia mused, "I suppose at any time, since I mean to put this aside for a few days."

"I will come for you tommorow afternoon," the baron offered promptly, "if the weather permits."

"Very well, John," Tonia said with a laugh. "As you see, I do not need much persuading."

145

The outcome of this conversation disturbed the Earl of Atlee profoundly. Here was yet another obstacle to interfere with his hope to monopolise Antonia and intensify his courtship. He was finding this daily contact with her tantalising but extremely unsatisfactory. The next morning he asked her to walk with him in the garden. With a feeling of sufferance she accepted, knowing that, before this interlude was over, she was going to have to refuse him again, despite the fact that she had been as circumspect as she could. She had hoped she could put off his declaration until another matter had been established on a firmer footing, realising he would never accept her refusal as final until she had announced her intention to marry someone else.

"Tonia, do you know this is the first time I have had you to myself since I arrived?" he said.

"Really, Robert?" she asked, feigning surprise. "I allow you are right, now I think on it. I did not imagine when I came here that there would be such a bustle. It is not much of a respite from the demands of the London Season, actually."

"I receive more of your attention in London than I do here," Atlee complained bitterly. "Tonia, must you go haring off to Ealand Hall?"

"Now Robert, you know that I reserve my summers for painting—usually in Dunstable and environs, it is true. But this is beautiful country, and I am excessively happy to be able to keep on with my work while I am here. I should like to paint something for the baron. He has a particular interest in art, and I am naturally pleased by his complimentary remarks."

Having also noticed a wayward yearning on that gentleman's part, and thinking to himself that the baron's judgement might be a little clouded, the earl, nevertheless, refrained from making any injudicious comment to that effect, realising that it could be misinterpreted as an adverse reflection on the merit of Tonia's work.

Touched by his downcast look, Tonia pressed his arm familiarly and coaxed, "Now do not take a pet, Robert. I will be around in the mornings and in the evenings, which I am persuaded is *quite* enough. We should likely become bored with each other if we were in each other's pockets the entire day."

"*I* would not," the earl declared staunchly. However, sensing the unresponsiveness of her mood, he reluctantly put off declaring himself and settled for the pleasure of her company until she insisted it was time for her to go to gather up her materials, since the baron would be coming for her very shortly.

From his study the duke watched them return to the house, looking for some indicating as to what may have passed between them. Observing that they seemed to be on their usual amiable terms, he concluded she had once again sidestepped the sensitive issue. It would have to be resolved soon, he decided peremptorily. Just as he had his problems, so she had hers. They both would have to clear the decks.

Tonia could not venture out every afternoon, for the weather continued to be infelicitous. On these dreary days the members of the household were hard put to find compatible amusements. They often took to pursuing their own interests, becoming dispirited with being housebound, an understandable reaction since the exodus to country estates in the summer was in great measure attributable to an expectation of enjoying outdoor pleasures.

During these weeks Lady Cecily had reached the unpalatable but inescapable conclusion that the duke would never consider making her his wife. In fact, it was obvious that he had no interest in her at all, having in a most reprehensible manner (considering that she was a guest, albeit uninvited) treated her with the barest civility. She had made the most grievous miscalculation when she had inveigled Lady Merrill into bringing her along and as a result she had exposed herself to this degraded standing in a group whose female members, except for Lady Merrill herself, she considered her social inferiors. Somehow she would have to extricate herself from an intolerable situation. With this purpose in mind she posted several letters to friends and relatives, announcing her whereabouts and complaining that she was sure if she were obliged to remain at Glenview much longer, she would die of boredom. She hoped that one or the other of these correspondents would come to her rescue and give her an excuse to effect a face-saving departure.

The third afternoon that Tonia spent at Ealand Hall working on her painting, the duke, returning from a trip to Southwell about the time she usually called it a day, decided to stop by for her. He was met by Alicia, who was delighted to see him. "Derek! How lucky that we can visit alone. I had so been looking forward to your return, and not yet have I had you to myself for a moment."

"I did not come to see you alone, Alicia," he told her bluntly.

"I am aware of that," the baroness acknowledged with a rueful expression. "I am not totally addlepated, you know. But we used to get on famously, and I miss our friendly exchanges. We have known each other forever, and I have always held you to be one of my very best friends."

"If you were content to leave it at that, Alicia, we could still be on good terms, because you are always excellent company. But I cannot support your foolishness, and so even our friendship is being put to a severe test. I was passing and have stopped to see how Tonia is progressing and to escort her back to the castle. Is she in the garden?"

"Yes. John went down a while ago to watch her work."

"Does he do that often?" Derek asked with a studied casualness.

"Oh, yes," the baroness replied complacently, failing to note the disapproval in his voice, in her anxiety to keep him with her. "They will appear shortly. She always stops about now. Do sit down and visit with me for a while. We will sit on the terrace, and I promise to behave with the utmost propriety."

The duke would have preferred to dash posthaste to the garden to interrupt Tonia and her admirer. But, not wanting to be obvious about making a piece of work of it, he resigned himself to accepting Alicia's invitation. Conversing amiably about their estates and some of his experiences on the Continent, they spent a pleasant half-hour reminiscing as old friends.

"It has been very enjoyable speaking with you without having to be on guard every moment, Alicia. I hope you will see fit to remember that," the duke remarked significantly. "But now I really must collect Tonia and return to the castle."

"It *has* been lovely, Derek. I can see there are definite advantages to being discreet," the baroness noted imprudently with a provocative smile.

The duke shot her a look of contempt and said harshly, "And so you have spoiled it, Alicia. You *are* addlepated"—a callous rejection that struck home even through the defenses of the determined baroness. For the first time she allowed herself to doubt the success of her amorous efforts and brooded that there must be a limit to just how much humiliation one should bring down on one's own head.

Derek reached the arched opening in the walled garden and came to an abrupt halt, trying to quell his rush of temper. Tonia was working with heedless concentration, but the baron, who had positioned himself to observe both the artist and her work, was so compromised by his undisguised look of admiration that the duke had a savage urge to plant him a facer. He set his jaw and with a supreme effort of self-control abruptly announced his presence. "Well, Tonia, do you mean to work until sundown?"

Both parties were startled by this sudden interruption—the baron, with a telling expression of guilt, which he quickly masked; and Tonia, with an exclamation of vexation.

"Derek! Look what you have made me do! You gave me such a start that I slipped with the brush," she scolded as she worked to correct the mistake. "What are you doing here?"

"I was driving nearby, and I decided to come bear you home," he told her coldly, outraged that she had the gall to take *him* to task when *her* conduct was much more answerable.

Hearing the anger in his voice, she knew she was in the basket, so she quickly gathered her materials and remarked peaceably, as she brushed her hair back from her face, "I had no idea it was so late. Will you store these for me until my next session, John?"

"Of course," the baron replied. "What do you think, Derek? I am quite pleased with Tonia's interpretation."

"Yes, it is very nice," the duke agreed curtly, commanding her with a scorching look to step lively.

Suspecting what had induced his fiery mood, which she found in no way repugnant, Tonia did not contest this demonstration of male dominance and allowed herself to be unceremoniously shepherded to Derek's curricle.

In his wrathful mood, he urged his horses to a fast pace, and Tonia found herself once again in danger of being dislodged from her seat.

"I begin to think you and Alicia might be meant for each other, after all," she charged, desperately holding on to her hat with one hand and to the side of the carriage with the other. "You both have an utter disregard for a passenger's comfort and mental tranquility."

He slowed the pair gradually, which unreasonably added to Tonia's resentment; to her it was evidence of the male's precious concern for the well-being of his horses over that of a mere human.

The duke pulled to a stop at the side of the road and turned to her with blazing eyes. "Just what the devil do you think you're doing?" he demanded.

"Hoping to come out of this perilous experience with my life," she replied irritably, as she straightened herself and began to smooth out her gown.

"Do not try to fob me off, you miserable baggage," Derek raged. "Have you lost your wits or are you really just an unconscionable flirt who must have all men dangling at her feet?"

"Good heavens! You *do* have a temper, don't you? Now I can appreciate why Colin was so disheartened after his acrimonious session with you," Tonia snapped.

"Tonia, my patience is wearing thin, and if you do not wish to find yourself being shaken forcibly, you had better explain yourself—to my satisfaction."

"I presume you are taking exception to my friendship with the baron?" she asked unblushingly.

"Friendship!" he exploded. "The man was practically grovelling at your feet."

"Derek!" Tonia exclaimed, truly shocked. "How dare you say such a thing? John has never said or done anything that was the least improper. I beg you will refrain from exaggerating the matter."

"You *do* admit to there being a matter?" he asked dangerously.

"Oh, well," she demurred lightly, "nothing serious."

"So *you* may think. I will grant you that much sensibility. But if you had seen his expression when I came upon you unexpectedly, you would put a different face on it."

Tonia looked at him in dismay. "Derek, surely you are mistaken. He may indulge in fantasies—it would not be unnatural, after all. But he could not be actually falling in love with me. He truly does love Alica, you know."

"Her behaviour can alter that case easily enough. There is a limit to what a man will endure."

"Yes, I know. That's why—" she began and then hesitated, deciding it might be better to postpone a confession, a scruple that was speedily put to rout when the duke commanded menacingly, "Go on."

"It is only that I like John very much, and I think it monstrous that so worthy a man must be embarrassed by an amorous wife who lusts after another man in such a disgustingly flagrant display. I hoped to shore up his self-esteem by showing him that he was still attractive and interesting to a woman—"

"My God, Tonia! How could you be so muddleheaded? Don't you know by now the effect you have on men? How did you expect to keep this harebrained scheme from getting out of hand?"

"For one thing, I expected Alicia to take note and claim her own," Tonia admitted frankly, and then added with a touch of resentment, "but she is so caught up by her delusions of seducing you that she cannot see the woods for the trees!"

"I have done everything I can to discourage her—you know that," the duke said defensively, feeling an acute discomfort at this frank exposition.

"Have you?" Tonia asked with her chin in the air. "Then how is it she is still giving chase?"

"What more would you have me do? I have cut her and told her candidly she was barking up the wrong tree, but she *is* deluded and refuses to listen."

"I'm sure *I* am not so presumptuous as to tell you how to manage your affairs, my lord," Tonia said self-righteously.

"The devil you aren't!" Derek retorted in amusement. "You have been leading me by the nose ever since I returned home. Now give over, Tonia. Let's discuss this calmly. Since you have initiated this little charade, I will take advantage of it by deliberately calling Alicia's attention to her husband's roving eye and suggesting she mend her fences before it becomes a habit with him."

"Very good, Derek," Tonia applauded with a grin, adding doubtfully, "but I do hope you will play down my part in it. Alicia is a good deal larger than I am, and I would not want to come to cuffs with her."

"I'll try to keep you out of the briars, you disgraceful imp. In the meantime I hope you will not encourage him further. He might be irreclaimable."

"All right," Tonia agreed with a shameless giggle, and then turned to him purposefully. "However, your grace, as long as we are speaking of false encouragement, you have a dilemma of your own making to resolve."

"What the devil is that supposed to mean? I have practically ignored Cecily's presence."

"Yes," Tonia acknowledged smugly, "you have made your sentiments perfectly clear there. I was speaking of Emily."

"Emily!" Derrick exclaimed incredulously. "She is a child. I am almost as old as her father."

"Yes, but I can assure you she does not look upon you as a *father,*" Tonia said.

"Good Lord! What else?" the duke groaned. "Surely she has not misinterpreted my manoeuvrings?"

"Surely she *has,*" Tonia told him. "What did you expect when you have been showering her with attentions and seeking her company so often? I understand that you used her to avoid Cecily, but Emily is still an innocent and did not realize what you were about."

"Not only to avoid Cecily," Derrick said meaningfully. "But I had no idea. Is Atlee aware of this?" he asked, thinking his friend would surely have set his daughter straight.

"I believe it is just becoming apparent to him, but he doesn't quite know what to do about it."

"What a muddle!" the chagrined gentleman remarked. "Well, we will clear up that matter, also. Now, since we are in a fair way to resolving my problems, I think we should address ourselves to yours."

"Mine?" Tonia asked with a sudden wariness.

"You know what I mean," the duke told her. "You are going to have to convince Robert that his suit is hopeless. You have let him dangle after you for five years, and he obviously still has aspirations. I know it has been convenient for you to have such a considerate, admirable gentleman at your beck and call," an accusation she could not deny because she knew she had found the earl's light-handed courtship advantageous, "particularly when he has been so undemanding. But the time has come for you to make an end to it."

With a deep sigh, Tonia said, "All right, Derek. But I am really very fond of Robert. It is going to be so difficult to be both firm and considerate. I do not wish to hurt him."

"I understand, Tonia. I regret the necessity, also. However, I'm sure you will find a way," the duke stated flatly.

She glared at him, taking little satisfaction from this encouragement, and suggested crossly, "It is getting very late. We had better hurry on."

"Yes" he agreed with a wicked grin. "Hold on, my girl. We will be there in a trice." With this abrupt warning he once again treated her to one of his famous rides, a demonstration she found totally unnerving. When he handed her down in the castle courtyard, she narrowed her eyes and announced, "I hope you derived some measure of satisfaction from that deplorable exhibition, your grace. But I beg you will not go out of your way to take me up again." And in indignation she stamped off, inflamed further by his immoderate burst of laughter.

That evening the duke refrained from favouring Emily, declining to participate in any of the games. He announced with a contrived languor (which almost put Tonia out of countenance considering his adolescent behaviour that afternoon) that it had unhappily come upon him he was not as young as he once was, and he begged to be excused as he felt uncommonly weary, a profession upheld when he stretched out lazily and closed his eyes. Though he seemed to sleep, Tonia once caught him looking at her mischievously through narrow slits, making her laugh at nothing, which caused the company to look at her questioningly and forced her to invent some ridiculous explanation for her lapse.

After a while he sat up and spoke to his stepmother. "Carla, I have been thinking it is time we started to make plans for our ball."

"Oh," Lady Merrill cried in pleasure, "I thought perhaps you had changed your mind."

"No, my dear, it's just that I haven't decided on a date. But you may start making up the guest list, preparing a menu, and planning decorations and entertainments. I know all that takes a little time. I will specify the day in a week or so."

"Certainly, Derek. Whom did you mean to invite?"

"Everyone, Carla. I cannot recall who all was standing about when I made my announcement so we will have to include everybody. Aunt Alvinia was there so perhaps you can ask her to help make the list."

"That will be a precious grand affair, Derek," Lady Carla commented doubtfully.

"I know, Carla, but we have a lot to celebrate, and we will share our pleasure with our friends and neighbours," he told her with a contented smile.

The next afternoon, determined to set in motion forces that would hasten ringing down the curtain on the final act of this ballooning comedy of errors, Derek once again appeared at Ealand Hall to have a private conference with Alicia.

She was surprised to see him, having almost convinced herself that her case was hopeless. But she quickly rejected that cheerless outlook and welcomed him with her usual bold manner.

"Alicia, *do* try to rid yourself of these tiresome postures. I have come to have a serious conversation with you, and I want you to concentrate on what I have to say and not be distracted by flights of fancy," the duke admonished sternly.

"Oh, dear, how solemn you are," the baroness said with some disappointment. "How is it that I had deluded myself into thinking you were an amiable man?"

"I am glad to hear you use that particular expression, Alicia. It gives me hope that you may be finally ready to throw over your absurd self-deception. I sincerely hope so because when I am married and am in residence here with my wife, I cannot be aggravated by your amorous advances nor," he added with a devilish grin, "do I think my duchess would for one moment countenance such an uncomfortable state of affairs."

"Married! Duchess!" the baroness cried in astonishment. "Derek, surely you are not going to marry that odious Cecily Mervyn! How could you do such a thing? Oh, I cannot bear it. To think of having that toplofty woman as a neighbour is beyond anything."

"Alicia, for God's sake! Will you stop raving? What kind of fool do you take me for? Of course I am not going to marry Cecily."

"Then whom?" she asked with a speculative eye. Suddenly, remembering his special attentions to Emily, she said in shock, "Good Lord! Not that *child*!"

"Alicia, I can see that you will not be satisfied until you know the whole. I will tell you if you promise to keep my confidence. Can I count on that?"

"Of course, Derek," the baroness replied eagerly. "You know I am always agreeable to hearing secrets."

"And keeping them," he prompted firmly.

"All right, Derek. I promise you I will keep quiet," she vowed, fully expecting him to admit to an intention of robbing the cradle, a design she deplored categorically, finding herself engaging in an unusual vilification of his character.

"I haven't proposed yet, you see. While the lady is well aware of my intentions, there are some matters to clear up first. But no, Alicia," he advised with a quizzical expression, "I am not going to rivet myself to a schoolgirl."

She looked at him searchingly and suddenly hit upon the incredible truth. "Tonia!" she ejaculated with a look of outrage. "Why, that miserable little slyboots! No *wonder* she tried to warn me off."

"Did she now?" Derek grinned. "And when, may I ask, did she do that?"

"When I drove her here to help with the ball," Alicia told him acidly. And then, unexpectedly, she burst out laughing—a joyous sound that seemed to signal some sort of release. "Very well, Derek. If it is to be Tonia, I know when I am beaten. She is an exceptionally redoubtable lady, though I admit I like her very well. In fact, I think we will be great friends."

"I think you will at that, Alicia," Derek agreed, "except that you may have temporary reservations."

"What do you mean?" she asked suspiciously.

"Well, I would not have to tell you if you had not been so preoccupied with your fantacising," the duke remonstrated. "But the fact is that John is halfway to being enamoured of Tonia."

Alicia stared at him incredulously, completely floored by this outlandish suggestion. She protested with a peculiar, defensive note in her voice, "John would *never* think of deceiving me. He is a thoroughly honourable man. You cannot really believe such poppycock!"

"I wouldn't have if I hadn't seen the evidence with my own eyes. But then, I had never met anyone like Tonia before, either."

"Derek, I *wish* you will stop mouthing such fustian," the baroness spouted irritably. "I am sure that John loves *me*."

"Yes, Alicia, I'm sure of that, too. And I believe that you love him, also, despite your determined indiscretion. But your recent behaviour has been disgraceful. It is no wonder that he would be attracted to a woman who shares his interests and makes him feel that she admires him as a worthy man. And, if you are still doubtful, think on it for a minute. How is it that Tonia came to help with the flowers? Who took her home? With whom does John spend most of his time when we are all together? Who asked her to do a painting? Who takes her to and from the hall? And, most incriminating of all, where does John spend his time when she is here? Where is he now?"

All of these provoking questions steadily built a convincing case for Derek's presumption. With an instantaneous impulse to rout the brazen temptress, Alicia rose abruptly and began to walk purposefully to the garden.

Derek grasped her arm and protested hastily, "Good Lord, Alicia, don't fly into a passion! Just what do you think you are going to do?"

"Unhand me, Derek," the enraged lady replied with blazing eyes. "I will tear that little hussy limb from limb! I'll teach her to be a husband-snatcher."

Appalled at the fury he had unleashed, the duke said coaxingly, "Now, do not go off half-cocked, Alicia. Sit here for a moment and listen to me." As he used considerable force, the baroness found herself once again seated on the terrace. "You have only yourself to blame, you know. And you are lucky that it is Tonia who has caught John's fancy. She would not permit the matter to become awkward. If it were someone else with fewer scruples, you might then have a problem. But the thing of it is, Alicia, this lapse has shown that John *is* vulnerable. And if it could happen once, there is nothing to say that it might not again. You might even consider that Tonia has done you a favour if it would make you realize what you were in danger of losing."

"A favour! That's putting a good face on it!" she fumed, though she had calmed down considerably.

He grinned at her teasingly, and she responded with a rueful smile." Isn't it strange?" she wondered aloud. "I never realised I felt like that. John has always been so kind and indulgent that I just took him for granted."

"Yes, Alicia. He really has an exceptionally gentle disposition, so you cannot expect him to play the lord and master. It is not his nature to be demanding."

"I know. I suppose that was part of my problem. However, it is not a one-sided thing, after all," she said with a most unladylike glint in her eye. "You may be sure I will not be so foolish again. As for Tonia—" she began, narrowing her eyes.

"Alicia," the duke objected whimsically, "I beg you will not do her violence. I would prefer my wife to be in fine feather on our wedding day, which I have every reason to hope will be very soon."

The baroness laughed at this. "When are you going to put it to the touch?"

"As soon as she resolves her situation with Atlee. I *do* have some scruples about proposing to my best friend's beloved, though, seeing as I unknowingly fell in love with Tonia the first day I met her, when I had no idea they were even acquainted, I do not really have any sense of guilt in the matter."

They heard Lord John and Tonia approaching then, and the duke pleaded, "Do control your temper, Alicia."

"Of course, Derek," she said blandly as she walked down to meet the pair. The duke followed after, prepared to rush to the rescue. But the baroness merely smiled lovingly at her husband as she grasped his arm possessively, throwing Tonia a challenging look. She asked pleasantly, "How did it go today? Now that you have gotten well into it, Tonia, I believe I shall join the two of you tomorrow to watch the artist at work. Perhaps I could learn something."

Understanding that Derek had enlightened Alicia and marvelling that she herself was still all in one piece, Tonia replied affably, "That would be excellent, Alicia. In fact, with your eye for colour and design, I would think that you could learn to paint rather well yourself."

"Perhaps I will try my hand at it. If nothing else I might better appreciate art and so be able to share John's interest," Alicia agreed promptly, favouring her husband with an amorous look. The baron was considerably confused by this obvious show of affection, and he wondered if the duke had dashed her hopes unequivocally, an interesting premise he rather hoped to have confirmed.

Once again finding herself escorted by the duke, Tonia was thankful that he seemed to be in a more mellow mood and did not feel impelled to drive like a madman. "I presume you apprised the baroness?"

"Yes. And only by brute force did I prevent her from trampling you underfoot," Derek told her wickedly. "However, luckily for you, she apparently intends to resolve the matter in a less savage manner. I believe John is going to be in for quite a surprise tonight."

"Derek!" Tonia protested, thinking this was just a *little* beyond what was acceptable, and amazed to find herself blushing under his laughing gaze. "Oh, you perfectly wretched man!"

=14=

TWO PLEASANT DAYS in a row seemed to call for an especially violent demonstration of Nature's capriciousness, and the household wakened the next morning to a particularly unpromising outlook. The ladies remained in their rooms quite late, taking time to perform sundry personal ministrations that were so much a tedium for the fairer sex.

One by one they all straggled down to breakfast but at no one time were more than four of them together. A mood of lethargy had spread throughout the castle, and all day long the confined inhabitants drifted lazily in and out of the various social rooms. In the early afternoon Derek came upon a trio in the billiard room. He quietly asked Julia, who was watching a match between Colin and Robert, where he could find Tonia.

"I don't know, Derek. She's not in her room or with Lady Alvinia. And she is certainly not outside." Then, remembering, she said with a chuckle, "Oh—" having lighted upon a probability.

"Yes," Derek replied with a grin, "very likely." With a wink he counselled, "Not a word, my dear," and a few minutes later he could be seen making his way towards his apartments in the west wing. Once there, however, he continued on to the back stairs and went down to the Long Gallery.

As he had expected, he found Tonia at her easel in front of the Raphael. The day was chilly, and she had a blanket across her lap and a shawl drawn around her shoulders, looking from behind very like a little old lady.

Derek laughed softly and greeted her with a provocative comment on her appearance, causing her to look at him forbiddingly as she said, "Did you come especially to insult me? How did you find me?"

"No, I did not. And I remembered your remark, when we were touring the castle, that should you seem to have disappeared, we would know where to look for you."

She acknowledged his remark with a little laugh and turned back to her canvas.

Derek came to examine her work, but she had not made a great deal of progress, having just started an hour before. "It is so dark that I cannot see very well," she complained.

"I will light the candles for you," he offered.

"No," she refused. "That would create unnatural shadows. It is much better to work in the daylight. I will just sketch today."

During the next hour or so, they talked easily of many things, making little probing inroads into each other's consciousness, both willingly revealing their innermost thoughts and convictions, setting the stage for their imminent final commitment.

Presently, when they both had reached a compelling state of suppressed excitement, kindled by their unspoken, undeniable passion for one another, Derek said commandingly with a revealingly urgent note in his voice, "Tonia, I would have you speak to Robert immediately. You have procrastinated long enough. I am impatient."

Not trusting herself to speak, as she was experiencing some unmaidenly yearnings herself, Tonia remained quiet for a moment and then replied softly, "Yes, Derek. I will do so. Perhaps not today, but tomorrow I will contrive a meeting with him."

He brought her hand to his lips and held it there possessively as he murmured teasingly, "Once again I will precede you to preserve your reputation. Do not remain long. It is too cold in here."

"No, I mean to pack up now. But I will go to my room for a few minutes and come down to tea a little later."

With a conspiratorial grin he bowed and left her to consider just how she was going to convince Robert that her decision was irrevocable. She would just have to tell him the truth, she decided. Nothing else would serve. And with this determination to take a straightforward approach, which must meet with success, she resigned herself to the inevitability of an uncomfortable interview.

The last few days Emily had gradually become aware of the duke's sudden change in manner. Though he was still pleasant, he was somehow more—avuncular. She began to suspect that she had misread his attentions, and she took herself to task without mercy. "Emily, whatever made you think that a man of the world like the duke, who is almost as old as your father (though she could still not see him in that light and admitted that in comparison her father seemed just a little bit stodgy), would have the least desire to pay court to you?" She should have been more discerning. It was obvious to her now, when she thought about it, that he was just trying to avoid being cornered by that odious Lady Cecily. What a ninnyhammer she was. It's a wonder Tonia didn't ring a peal over her. She hoped she hadn't made a perfect fool of herself. Well, Emily told herself, she would chalk this folly up to experience and would try to remember to be more standoffish. She had learned a good deal since she came to Glenview, but she understood she had a lot more growing up to do before she could hope to acquire the serenity of spirit and self-confidence that Julia and Tonia possessed in such good measure. She would speak to Tonia and tell her she recognised her mistake. "After all, I do not want her to imagine that she would have to spend the whole of next Season worrying about what maggot I would next get in my head." Having thus ruthlessly expunged her youthful fancies, she proceeded to spend the evening turning to account an observing eye, verifying her conclusions and making some startling new ones.

Tonia knew she only had to make herself available to have Robert seek her exclusive company, so she casually joined the rest of the household the next morning and waited for him to approach her. Within minutes she found herself strolling with him in the garden, accepting that she must jump this last hurdle before she and Derek could begin making plans for their future.

"Tonia," Robert began, "there are circumstances which make it desirable for Emily and me to quit Glenview. I cannot bear to leave you, however, without trying once more to convince you to be my wife. I do love you deeply, Tonia, and I am so pleased that you and Emily are in harmony with one another. I have not seen nearly enough of you while we have been here, but even so, it has been extremely gratifying to have you near every day. My dear, will you not make me the happiest man in the world and accept my proposal?" he pleaded, taking her hands and looking ardently into her eyes, clearly revealing the depths of his feelings so that Tonia was struck with guilt and compassion and felt she could not possibly go through with it. Still, visualising that reprisals might befall her if she did not follow instructions, she took a deep breath and pulled him over to sit on a bench.

"Robert, because I am extremely fond of you, I am finding it very difficult to have to tell you that what you want can never be. I should have been firmer in my refusals before because I have known all along that I could not marry you."

"Why, Tonia?" he asked desperately. "We—"

"Hush, my dear," she said as she put her hand on his lips. "You see, I'm afraid I am an incurable romantic. Perhaps that seems foolish at my age, but I have never given up hope of finding a man whom I would love in that special way. Always in the back of my mind was the dreadful vision of seeing myself wed to someone for whom I merely felt affection and then too late finding my true love. What could I do then, Robert? The prospect of lifelong unhappiness was insupportable. I could not chance it. Yet I knew that you were deeply committed and would not stop hoping until I accepted someone else, so I gave up trying to dissuade you. But Robert—I tell you this in the strictest confidence because we have not yet spoken openly of the matter—I *have* found my love, and I have the happy expectation of being married very shortly."

The earl looked at her in shock, having been totally unprepared for such a crushing blow. He closed his eyes and sat back, trying to absorb what she had told him. It was no use. He could not believe it. "Tonia, I had no idea. How could this be? Did you meet someone in London? Why didn't you tell me?"

"Robert," she said desperately, beginning to feel oppressed, "the *hardest* part is having to tell you that Derek and I, behind our squabbling, are really very much in love with one another."

"Derek! My God!" Robert groaned, putting his head in his hands. Then, in anger, he muttered bitterly, "So! He has cut me out—"

"Robert," Tonia said, hurrying to defend the duke before his friend should conceive the wild notion of calling him out, "it is not like that at all. Actually, it hit us almost immediately, though, of course, neither of us would have admitted it if we had been boiled in oil. Derek had no idea you and I even knew each other. And after you came, he realised that I never had any intention of accepting you. Still, he has not actually proposed yet. We have been exercising our wits and engaging in considerable fencing, directing each other to clear the way," she said with a grin. "And much as it might seem forward of me to be so confident, I had to tell you beforehand so you would not make a piece of work of it when it comes out into the open."

The earl began pacing back and forth as he asked, "Why didn't I see it? Does anyone else know?"

"I suspect Julia, Colin, and Lady Alvinia have guessed," Tonia replied, "but then they were all here when we first met so could recognise the early signs."

"And so that's the end of it," he said miserably, looking at her with undisguised longing.

"Yes, Robert. I *am* sorry. I should never have let it go on so long," she told him unhappily.

Becoming aware of her brimming eyes, he realised she really was deeply distressed, and he pulled her into his arms to hold her tightly. "My love, do not blame yourself. You did refuse me five times. And you are right in thinking I would never have stopped trying as long as you were free. I will have to try to bring myself to swallow this truly bitter pill. I will never stop loving you, you know. I hope Derek is going to be complaisant about that, because I cannot bear to think of not seeing you from time to time."

"Well," she said sternly, relieved that he appeared resigned, "I *hope* you do not mean to make yourself a stranger. How dreadful it would be if you and Derek should be so buffleheaded as to sacrifice your friendship because of a mere female."

He had to laugh, and, putting his hand under her chin, he tilted her head and bent to kiss her, an exercise to which a gentleman took strong exception in the privacy of his study where he stood at the window. "That shameless Jezebel! What kind of a refusal is that? And it's not the first time, either," he judged, narrowing his eyes. "She is much too cooperative." Still seething, Derek watched as the two figures drew apart, not the least ashamed of his spying, having convinced himself that he was justified in keeping his eye on that little devil who obviously had been running unchecked too long and was sadly in need of a strong hand.

"Thank you, Tonia," the earl said gently. "That will have to last me a lifetime. You will forgive me if I don't remain to join in the forthcoming celebrations? I don't think I will be quite up to it. This is going to take a little getting used to, I'm afraid."

"I understand, Robert," she said softly.

"Besides," he continued thoughtfully, "it would be best to remove Emily from Glenview. I believe she has been following in my footsteps and has set her sights on an unlikely candidate."

"I think she is over that, Robert. It will not be a problem," Tonia assured him.

"Well, in any case, we shall leave. I will go now to break the news to her. I *do* wish you happy, Tonia," he said sincerely.

"Thank you, dear Robert," Tonia replied gratefully as she raised herself to kiss his cheek, further incriminating herself in the eyes of a self-proclaimed nemesis. The earl left her then, and she remained in the garden, breathing a sigh of relief that the deed was done, and thankful that it had been easier than she had expected.

=15=

THOUGH HE FELT emotionally drained and desperately bluedeviled, the earl kept himself resolutely under control, determined not to make a fool of himself. Nevertheless he experienced an urgent need to get away. It would take some time to come to terms with the reality of Derek's part in this. Though Robert could not completely quell his feeling of rancor against his friend, it had been somewhat subdued by Tonia's exculpatory acquittal. No more than Derek could he wish to break off their longstanding friendship. And so, he would leave at once to give himself time to try to make the best of it. With the intention of explaining to Emily that they must return to Altee Hall, he proceeded to the drawing room where he knew she was sitting with Lady Alvinia, watching her work on her needlepoint tapestry.

"Oh, hello, Papa," the girl greeted him brightly. "Look! Can you imagine that Lady Alvinia has been working on this for forty years! Isn't it beautiful?"

"Yes, my dear, it certainly is," Lord Robert agreed. "How far are you, Lady Alvinia?" he asked, glad for the diversion from his own heavy thoughts.

"Just one generation back now," she replied. "It is nearly finished."

"There will be another generation, you know," he remarked with a pained smile. "You will never really be finished." Turning to his daughter, he said, "Emily, I have come to see if I could persuade you to go for a drive with me. It is a lovely day, and we could stop for lunch somewhere."

"Why, Papa," the girl responded with a surprised smile, "that would be famous! Do you have an errand?"

"No, my dear. I have something I want to talk over with you, and I thought a drive would be pleasant."

"All right. I'll get my bonnet and be ready in a few minutes," she called over her shoulder as she hurried away, thinking he wished to explain to her about the duke and being thankful that she had already quashed *that* flight of fancy.

A few minutes later they were tooling down the driveway in Derek's curricle. The earl turned to his daughter to say, "You look very lovely in that bonnet, Emily. Overnight you have become a beautiful young lady. I am very pleased that here at Glenview we have begun to know one another better even though there are many others around."

"Oh, Papa, do you feel that way, too?" Emily cried, blushing with pleasure. "I am so glad that I don't have to go back to school. I would much rather stay with you. And it has been so pleasant here, especially being friends with Julia and Tonia. I do mean to try to be like them, you know," she said with an eloquent expression.

"Do you, my dear?" the earl asked with a smile. "Well, since you are so attached to them, I wonder if you will object when I tell you that I think it is time for us to leave."

"Oh," Emily said blankly, as she looked at her father regretfully, unable to hide her disappointment. Imagining that her foolish infatuation had evoked this decision, she quickly spoke up to allay his misgivings. "Papa, if you think that I have formed a *tendre* for the duke, you need not mind that, ,because I realize I misunderstood and have quite censured myself for being such a gudgeon. So we do not have to go on that account," she said hopefully.

The earl smiled at her with affection. "It was not only that, my dear, though I am glad you have perceived your mistake on your own. It shows you are properly refining your discrimination. And since you have been so open with me, Emily, I shall do you the same honour. You know, of course, that I have loved Tonia these five years and more. I have asked here to marry me many times but she has always refused me. Today she convinced me that my case was hopeless. So in order for me to get used to the idea, I thought it would be better to go away for a while."

"Oh, Papa, I am so sorry," Emily commiserated, her eyes filling with sympathetic tears. "Is it—is it becaue she is going to marry the duke?"

The earl pulled the carriage to a stop a little off the road and turned to his daughter with a wondering look. "How did you know that?"

"I don't know precisely, Papa. But they always seem to understand one another. I mean, when they speak to each other, it sounds perfectly normal but—oh, I don't know. I noticed it particularly last night. It is almost as though they don't have to speak to know what the other is thinking. I thought, 'That must be how it is when people are in love.' And I suddenly knew that was the case with them."

"You are very observant, Emily. I didn't see it myself," the earl confessed ruefully.

"Papa," the girl said, reaching out to grasp his hand, "I know how terribly disappointed you must be. And much as I would wish you happy and would like to have Tonia for my mother—though I have to say I could not really think of her like that, for she doesn't act like any mother I have ever seen—I could not wish for you to be married to a lady who is in love with another man. It would be dreadful for both of you."

"You are a good pupil, Emily," Lord Robert commended her with a wry look. "That is precisely the reason she has put me off all these years—becuase she still thought that one day she would find her love."

"And she was right, Papa," Emily admonished gently.

Looking keenly at this daughter who seemed to have suddenly acquired a deep sensibility beyond her years, he unexpectedly conceived an idea that he decided to put to her immediately.

"Emily, I wonder how set you are on having a Season next year," he ventured.

With a quick look of dismay, which she tried to disguise by lowering her eyes, the girl asked with a suspicious quaver, "Do you think Tonia will not wish to present me, after all?"

"No, my dear, I don't think that, though there is a strong

168

chance, you know," he noted meaningfully, "that it might not be convenient for her."

"Oh," Emily gasped with quick comprehension, confirming her rapid progression toward maturity. "I hadn't thought about *that* yet."

Not wishing to pursue further a subject to which he had a strong aversion, the earl offered another persuasion. "You will only have just turned seventeen next April. It would not be at all inopportune if we were to postpone it one year, and I'm sure Tonia will keep her promise even then. You need not worry about that. But, considering everything, I hope you will agree with me that it would be best to wait. In fact, while we have been talking, another proposition has been forming in my mind. How would you like to make a tour of the Continent with me?"

"A Grand Tour?" Emily exclaimed with an awed expression.

"A *very* grand one," the earl replied with a smile. "I have often pored over the accounts of notable earlier travelers—Edward Gibbons, Mrs. Hester Piozzi, Sir Thomas Nugent, and several others—and I admit to having had burning ambitions to follow their footsteps. But the wars with Napoleon unhappily precluded any such venture. And since I was assigned to the Home Office, I never had even a taste of it. So! What are your thoughts? Would you consider indulging your father in one of his boyhood fancies?"

Emily had to laugh at his wistful expression, and she embraced him fiercely. "Papa, I think that is the most famous plan. And by the time we come back, perhaps I will have learned to be more discerning, so that I am not so susceptible to a gentleman's gallantry."

The earl smiled at this ingenuous observation, remarking with satisfaction, "I am very pleased you are receptive, Emily. It will not always be comfortable, you know. Travelling can be very tedious, though I am persuaded that it will not be the hard road it was fifty years ago. Besides, I have many acquaintances abroad. We will not always have to put up at hotels or inns."

"Oh, I shall not mind that, Papa. I'm sure it is going to be the greatest adventure. How long will we stay? Where will we go?"

"As long as you wish and wherever you like—France, Italy, Greece, Switzerland—"

"And perhaps meet Lord Byron?" Emily asked impishly.

"Perhaps," the earl agreed with an indulgent smile.

"When will we leave?"

"Well, it will take a little time to make arrangements, but I think a month might be a good estimate. In the meantime we will go to Atlee Hall to organize our affairs for a long absence."

With a happy sigh Emily sat back to contemplate this totally new and wonderfully surprising idea, thinking how exciting the next few years promised to be. "When do we leave Glenview?" she asked.

"The day after tomorrow, if it is all right with you."

"Of course, Papa. We have so much to do. When we go back this afternoon, I will tell Tonia."

The earl nodded in agreement and once again picked up the reins to continue their drive to Southwell. They lunched at the Saracen's Head Inn while he teasingly recounted some of the experiences that could befall them, though Emily would not be daunted, pronouncing herself as hardy as any female and declaring that since others had weathered such a journey, *she* certainly could.

They returned to the castle in the late afternoon, having found themselves wholly pleased with each other, both firmly convinced that they would do very well together. The earl, now being more quiescent, his mood having been softened by this happy *tête-à-tête* with his daughter, went directly to Derek's study to announce his decision to quit Glenview.

By this time the duke had managed at least to subdue his resentment of the two parties involved in the intimate scene that had put him on his mettle, partly because he had avoided Tonia and thus was not provoked into some indiscretion, so he was able to greet his friend with only the slightest nettled note in his voice. "I hear you and Emily deserted the company this afternoon."

"Yes, I wanted to talk to her and had my eyes opened considerably, I can tell you. Derek, that child has grown up overnight. She has a great deal of sense—and sensibility. I know I am likely prejudiced, but I believe she is becoming quite an exceptional young lady."

Derek had to laugh at this sudden burst of parental pride. "I don't think you will find any argument there, Robert," he agreed. "Emily has a great charm and a lively sense of humour. She will certainly be a belle, as Tonia has prophesied."

"But not next year," the earl advised firmly. "We talked today because I wanted to break it to her that it was time to leave. We were both inviting a failure of expectation."

"I'm sorry about that, Robert," the duke apologized humbly. "I was extremely careless. It just never occurred to me that she would misunderstand. I was very much at fault."

"Well, if I hadn't been so preoccupied, I would have set her straight at the first signs. However, it is of no matter. Before I could broach the subject, she brought it up and informed me she had worked it out for herself. And though it might offend your vanity, I am happy to say that she did not seem the least cut up about it."

Derek gave a crooked smile and asked, "Why do you say that she will not have a Season next spring?"

"Well, Emily is very young, and I was able to convince her that to wait one year would be better, especially since I held out the lure of a Grand Tour."

Derek laughed. "You always did have a yen for that. But how is it you suddenly decided to go now?" he asked.

"Today Tonia refused me again," the earl reluctantly told his rival with a deep sigh of resignation, "but this time she left me without a hope. It hit me pretty hard, actually. I realize now I had always thought she would agree to marry me eventually. And since I must begin trying to accustom myself to this unexpected blow, I decided I must put some distance between us for a while. Though," he added defiantly, turning to face the duke squarely, "I shall always love her."

171

Derek unwaveringly returned his challenging look, and then, having a sudden sympathy for his heavyhearted friend, he put down his hostility and acknowledged peaceably, "I understand, Robert."

With what seemed an expression of relief, the earl advised brusquely, "We will leave for Atlee Hall the day after tomorrow to make plans."

Derek moved to clasp him on the shoulder in the manner of friends and pronounced, "I appreciate your having accompanied me on my rounds this spring, Robert. We have always been good comrades. When you return to England, I hope we will again see you at Glenview."

"You can count on that," the earl told him with a crooked grin.

Emily had immediately inquired for Tonia and was disappointed to learn that she had not yet returned from Ealand Hall. Julia and Colin, too, were off on an excursion of their own. Consequently, by the time she was able to unburden herself, she was fairly bursting with her news.

So it was that when Tonia arrived back at the castle, after having spent a curious afternoon in the walled garden with two individuals who behaved every bit like a pair of newlyweds, she found herself unceremoniously pounced upon by a very impatient young lady.

"Tonia! I have been waiting to talk with you. You are so late!" Emily cried, her eyes sparkling with excitement.

"My dear girl, whatever has sent you into transports?" Tonia asked in amusement, a little surprised at her reaction. She could not imagine that Emily would be overjoyed to learn that her father had been dealt a crushing blow.

"Oh, *wait* 'til you hear. You will never guess!"

"In that case you had better tell me. But come to my room so that I can begin removing the paint."

They entered Tonia's room, and Emily immediately plopped herself on the bed to announce dramatically, "Tonia, you will not have to present me next Season, after all!"

"I won't?" Tonia asked with a startled expression.

"No. I *am* rather young and *much* too impressionable, so I have decided to wait another year," the girl confided artlessly.

"You have?"

"Yes. You see, Papa and I were talking and—"

"Emily," Tonia ventured with a sinking presentiment, "I hope you are not going to tell me that your father has been indiscreet."

"No, Tonia, he didn't tell me. I guessed."

"You did?"

"Yes. It came to me last night when I was watching everyone. It was so obvious that I don't know why I didn't notice it before."

"It was?" Tonia asked, seeming to have lost her conversational facility.

"Yes. It suddenly came to me that you treated the duke differently from other gentlemen. I mean, with Papa, Colin and the baron you are always amiable and interested and teasing, but with the duke you—oh, I don't know exactly—it is almost as though—as though you were playing a game with each other," she declared triumphantly as she realized she had unwittingly hit upon the true nature of their relationship.

Tonia laughed delightedly. "Emily, you are a little minx. How in the world did you grow so awake on all suits so fast?"

"I don't know, though it must have happened suddenly," the girl said with an uncertain frown, "for I surely was not all that perceptive during the last few weeks, when I entertained fantasies about the duke."

"Well, you can hardly be blamed for that," Tonia told her. "He was regrettably unmindful."

"I *should* have known better."

As the girl was obviously in the mood for holding herself to account, Tonia let the matter rest. "Emily, you do not imagine that I would not wish to present you because of the way things have turned out?"

"No, Tonia," Emily replied hastily. "I haven't *told* you yet. Papa and I are going to make a Grand Tour!"

"You are?" Tonia asked in astonishment.

"Yes! Papa has always wanted to, and we are going together. Isn't that famous? And we may even see Lord Byron!"

"Emily, I think that is a perfectly marvelous idea!" Tonia applauded. "I am excessively jealous. Why, you are going to be so cosmopolitan when you come back, you will certainly outshine the other young ladies."

Emily laughed merrily and teased, "Perhaps the duke will take you sometime."

"Perhaps," Tonia agreed with a little smile.

"And do not think I will release you from your promise to sponsor me," Emily warned her. "But you will have your work cut out for you, you know. I have already had to give up two exceptional gentlemen to you and Julia, so you will have to find another *nonpareil* for me. I certainly do not mean to settle for an inferior specimen."

"Not to worry, my love. You will have your pick and will be in luck if you just make the right choice. *That* can be very ticklish. But, in fact, I do have a capital candidate in mind," Tonia announced teasingly as she suddenly thought of her beloved cousin, Aunt Margot's eldest son, now Baron Walton.

"Really, Tonia?" Emily asked eagerly. "Tell me who he is."

"Certainly not. You will have to find him for yourself. Then you will know for sure."

"With *my* luck he will probably be snapped up before I have a chance to bait him," Emily mourned.

Tonia burst out laughing and embraced her young friend affectionately. "I will try to save him for you," she promised.

Julia came in then and, being immediately apprised of this late development, unequivocally offered her stamp of approval. "Why, Emily, you are a very lucky girl," she said congratulating her. "You must keep a diary so that you will remember everything and be able to keep us entertained for years."

"That *will* be great fun," Emily cried. "Oh, I am so excited. I can hardly wait. I will send you a letter from every place I visit. And I *hope* you will write to me."

174

"Yes, my love, we most certainly will," Tonia assured her and then showed her the door so they might all dress for dinner.

All that evening the conversation centred around the newly formed plans, for Emily had produced a notebook and relentlessly queried the duke, Colin, and Lord and Lady Merrill about what they had seen and what she and her father should not miss. She was so animated and charmingly curious that they all indulged her, entertaining even those who had not travelled abroad and had no immediate prospects to do so. At midnight the earl finally rang down the curtain on his daughter's enthusiasm, saying she might have to put off her Season for two years if she meant to explore every site with a pretension to fame between England and Greece.

"Yes, Emily," Tonia affirmed teasingly. "I do hope you will be back a month or so before the Season begins so we will have time to make plans."

"Don't worry, Tonia. I am looking forward to playing our game," the girl replied significantly, and intentionally left the rest of the company in ignorance as to what she meant by that cryptic statement.

In her room, as she was getting ready to retire, the Countess of Falmouth took stock of several discoveries she had made that evening. She cared little if Robert and his daughter took off on a Grand Tour, except that it suggested Antonia had refused him again and that he had finally come to accept it. This surmise was borne out, as he seemed to have scrupulously kept a distance between them that evening. But what inauspiciously opened Lady Cecily's eyes was the fact that Derek had usurped the position next to Antonia that Robert usually managed to reserve for himself. The implication of this subtle reversal added fuel to the flame. If she had felt a mild antagonism towards the lady before, she now held her in intense dislike. Always the popular Miss Radcliffe had been a thorn in her side, but in snaring the most eligible bachelor in England, she had invited an added store of ill will. As the countess seethed inwardly, she decided she had best leave immediately before an announcement was made. The only response she had had to her numerous letters came from her former husband's nephew, who had been his heir and was now the Earl of Falmouth. He was only two years older than she and had been widowed a year ago when his wife died giving birth to their third child, a second son. He had been making advances for some time, and Lady Cecily knew what role he had in mind for her, a position she had always resisted. But now, having failed to attach the marquess or the duke, she speculated whether she might not be able to bring him up to scratch. Marrying her husband's nephew would certainly shock society and expose her to censure. Nevertheless, other uncommon matches had been made and accepted eventually. It was worth a try anyway. This existence as a merry widow was becoming extremely unsatisfactory. One must have a husband to cut a swath in the *ton*. And a husband she would get.

With the purpose of setting the stage for her departure, the countess joined the others for breakfast at nine o'clock. Feigning regret, she spoke familiarly to the duke. "Derek, it has been so pleasant here at Glenview, but I'm afraid I must make plans to leave immediately. I have received a letter from dear Randolph, asking for my assistance. He has been trying to make arrangements for his little ones and is having trouble finding a proper nanny." She gave a little laugh and confided, "He sounds dreadfully up against it, so I feel I must rush to his rescue."

Lady Carla's sympathetic nature once again surfaced. "Oh, my dear Cecily," she said, "that would be excessively kind of you. I'm sure he must find it extremely trying. Imagine having three motherless children all under six years!"

"Well, Cecily, if you will tell me when you wish to leave, I will order the travelling carriage readied for you," "the duke offered gallantly, perfectly amenable to allowing her her pretensions, feeling extremely relieved she had chosen to depart on her own. "My coachman and one of the grooms can escort you to Falmouth Park and make arrangements for your night on the road."

Lady Cecily accepted readily, privately gloating on what an impression she would make bowling around the countryside in a ducal carriage. With a smug calculation, she visualised her arrival at her destination, hoping fervently that Falmouth would be there to remark it.

That afternoon several of Glenview's inhabitants gathered for a shopping excursion to Nottingham. Searching determinedly in the bookstores, Julia and Tonia finally found a gold-tooled leather diary for Emily to take on her journey. Derek and Colin followed the same line, buying her guide books to study before she left. Lady Carla was of a more practical mind and presented her with a little jewelry bag that could be tied around her waist, since she had learned from experience that one should keep valuables on one's person at all times. After a festive lunch in town, they returned to the castle to rest before dressing for their farewell dinner.

=16=

THERE WAS A great deal of bustle in the castle the next morning as last minute preparations were made for departure. Two carriages were drawn up before the front entrance and were being loaded with baggage.

Emily sat talking quietly with Tonia and Julia, suddenly feeling reluctant to leave them after so short an acquaintance.

"Emily, my dear," Tonia said consolingly, touched by the young girl's attachment to them, "the time will fly by. Before you know it, you will be back with us, ready to take the *ton* by storm."

"Oh, I know," Emily allowed ingenuously. "It's just that everything has been happening so fast lately that I never seem to have time to enjoy one new experience before I am off on another."

The two ladies laughed and embraced her affectionately as the earl came to say his farewells. He kissed both sisters on the brow and told them he would bring Emily back to them in due time. Then, with a last warm look for Tonia, he walked away to await his daughter at the carriage. With unbidden tears, Emily once again threw her arms around her friends, whispering to each of them that she wished them happy. The earl helped her into the carriage, and they were on their way, Emily leaning out of the window, waving until she could no longer see the castle.

Derek had moved to stand next to Tonia, and he was surprised to see a tear trickle down her cheek. He said softly, "You will have me believing that you are sorry to have sent him away."

"It isn't that. But I think I must have caught Emily's nostalgia. When things change so dramatically and so quickly, it takes a little getting used to. I almost feel that part of my life has just taken flight. And then, I have become very fond of Emily. I believe I am going to miss her."

"I doubt that," the duke said flatly, favouring her with an intimate look before he turned to help his other departing guest into the travelling carriage.

"Thank you, Derek," Lady Cecily said. "I am sure I will be very comfortable. I am excessively glad I did not have to hire a chaise." She sat back immediately, not wishing to observe the duke and Antonia standing together, giving an impression that the little schemer was already mistress there. This unpalatable probability put the countess in a temper, which she vented on her mettlesome maid. That young woman turned a deaf ear as she sorrowfully dwelt on the turns of Fate that befell her, forcing her departure before she had had a chance to attach the young footman. She speculated whether one of the Misses Radcliffe would be needing a new abigail.

With this second departure the household began to disperse to attend to various personal concerns. Colin and Julia asked the duke and Tonia if they would care to join them for a ride, but Tonia refused, saying she would be going to Ealand Hall shortly.

"The devil you will!" Derek exploded.

"Just what do you mean by that?" she asked challengingly. "It is a lovely day. John will likely be coming for me soon."

"We will send him a note telling him you are busy today."

"Really, Derek, I must say you are being excessively high-handed," Tonia complained indignantly. "I do not have other plans."

"Well, I do. We are going for a walk—just the two of us. Now that we have finally disposed of all inhibiting, extraneous matters, we are going to settle things between us," the duke told her confidently.

"I am not at all aware of—" Tonia began haughtily, taking exception to his lordly manner.

The duke interrupted her, stating firmly, with a dangerous glint in his eye, "Antonia, if you wish to change your shoes and get a bonnet, you may do so. Otherwise, you may come as you are. But you *are* coming."

Realizing that any further hesitation on her part would only make her defeat more pronounced and not really being reluctant, Tonia elected to protect her dignity. "Oh, very well!" she said grudgingly, "if you *must* have your own way," and turned on her heel to go to collect her things, leaving an irreverently amused trio.

When she came back downstairs, Derek smiled happily and took her by the hand. They wandered leisurely through the park, speaking very little, both anticipating the moment when they would declare their love.

At the little temple they turned to face one another and embraced. Derek tightened his arms and murmured passionately, "I love you to distraction, Tonia. I want desperately to marry you. I have wanted so much to tell you how I feel, but I did not dare declare myself until you had dismissed Robert. I did not want to irreparably damage our long friendship, and I knew that once I had held you in my arms, discretion would be thrown to the winds. So I set myself a damnable trial and forced myself to wait." As the kiss he pressed on her lips convincingly demonstrated his depth of feeling, Toni considered it only proper to lend her full cooperation.

Some time later Derek brought himself under control, but continued to hold her as he buried his face in her hair. "You are so incredibly enchanting, Tonia. I confess myself hopelessly enslaved. I hope you will be kind to me."

"Derek, you are doing this awfully well," Tonia commended breathlessly as she brushed her lips against his, which invited him to resume his amorous activities. Presently he held her a little away and looked at her commandingly. "My love, though you have responded very nicely, you have not yet said you mean to marry me."

"Oh, well," she began, in another of her mischievous starts, "I am sure I had quite made my mind up to that before I had even met you, being so favourably impressed by Colin, you know, and thinking how lovely it would be to be doubly related. And then," she continued, wholly undaunted by the warning glint in his eyes, "when Mama reproved me for my extravagance, I decided there was nothing for it but to marry a wealthy duke. It became a settled thing, of course, after I had seen Glenview."

"Tonia," Derek said warmly, "if you do not stop offering provocation, you will certainly pay the piper, for I have been wanting to do you violence from that very first day, when you stood at the library door looking at me as though I were some sort of oddity."

She laughed and took his face in her hands. "All right, my darling, I will do it properly. I do love you, Derek. I have felt so happy since I have been here. Of course I mean to marry you. I have never wanted anything so much."

Finding this highly satisfactory submission totally unmanning, Derek once again uninhibitedly indulged his own ardour which Tonia returned wholeheartedly.

"Tonia, why did you not come to me sooner? We have wasted so much time!"

"Really, Derek, how dare you hold me to account!" she protested indignantly. "Every spring these last twelve years I have gone to London to look for you, and you never once thought to come find me!"

"Grassed again," the duke said ruefully. "We shall blame it on the war, my love. But we have waited long enough. I will get a special license so that we may be married at once. Will your parents be agreeable to coming to Glenview in a few days time?"

"I imagine so, if properly tempted," she judged with a twinkling eye.

"I shall send a letter with a rider tomorrow and will also inform Carla to have the invitations delivered. Then I will ride off to find us a bishop who can issue a special license."

"Very efficient, your grace," Tonia applauded.

"It isn't as though I haven't been thinking about it," he replied, kissing her soundly. "Come, it's getting late. They will be sending out a search party."

"Oh, dear," Tonia murmured, as she felt several loose strands curling about her face and neck. "Should I appear in such a disheveled state, anyone would know I had been thoroughly compromised."

"Nothing like it," Derek said. "Just tuck in the loose ends, and the squirrel's nest will be intact again."

Tonia giggled at this ostensibly derogatory remark and merely followed his suggestion before putting on her bonnet, which helped hide the evidence. "Derek, before you send off the letter to Mama and Papa, I would like to add a short note."

"A tempter?" he asked as he placed his arm around her waist.

"I suppose you could say that," she replied, dimpling prettily.

Tonia was sitting at her dressing table taking down her hair when Julia came in to discover if everything had been happily resolved. Seeing her sister's mischievous face she knew that Tonia at least was satisfied with the results. She asked, "Did you have a pleasant afternoon?"

"Yes, love," Tonia replied dreamily. "I must tell you that you will have to accept the fact that I shall precede you to the altar, after all."

"Oh, Tonia, I am *so* pleased. I have known it would work out like this. Derek has been quite open about it, and I knew you meant to have him. Isn't it the luckiest thing that we should make such close connexions? When is it to be?"

"As soon as Mama and Papa can be persuaded to come. Derek is quite determined about that. Really, Julia, I am likely bruised all over from having been so thoroughly mauled. I do hope," she said with a reproving look, "that you do not permit Colin to take such liberties. It is *most* improper!"

This admonition sent Julia into a spasm of laughter, and she plopped helplessly on the bed with tears running down her face as she gasped, "Tonia, you are the most outrageous girl. I was going to miss you dreadfully, though I knew our separation had to come eventually. Now everything will be perfect. We shall certainly be often together."

"Yes, Julia, I am glad for that, too," Tonia confided as she joined her on the bed, hugging her happily. "I admit to having felt lower than I showed, though I *had* hoped a maiden aunt might be in demand." After several more moments of optimistic discussion on their incredibly good fortune, they called for their maid to help them dress for dinner.

When the family met in the drawing room, Lady Carla looked at Tonia in bewilderment. "My dear, I was so surprised that Robert decided to leave. I had thought the two of you would finally make a match of it. Surely you did not send him away!"

"She most certainly did, Carla," Derek announced categorically. "I positively insisted she do so. I mean to marry her myself, you know, and I definitely did not want one of her moonstruck suitors hanging around."

Lady Carla stared at her stepson with her mouth open, completely nonplussed. She looked helplessly at her husband who, also taken by surprise, quickly recovered himself and congratulated the couple warmly. Lady Carla began to stammer, "But how—when—oh, dear, I cannot credit it. I had no idea!"

"You were just not looking for it, Mother," Colin informed her. "And Robert's presence served to disguise the truth."

"Well, I do not mean to seem displeased about it," Lady Carla reassured him, hoping she had not given the impression that she had not yet accepted Derek's dictum. "I was just caught unaware. I do wish you happy, Derek, truly I do." She then embraced Tonia and remarked how fortuitous it was that they would all be one big family "...for I do think we have rubbed along very well together."

"Yes, Lady Carla," Tonia agreed, "so we have. And Julia and I consider ourselves very fortunate to have such happy prospects before us."

Derek moved to put his arm around her and pulled her next to him. "So now, Carla," he advised, "you may send out the invitations for a week from now. I think everything should be in order then for announcing our engagement. Two days later Tonia and I will be married in the morning in the chapel."

Lady Alvinia added her wholehearted approval, and smiled

gratefully when Tonia made a point of remarking that she was certainly glad she would have a resident mentor to help her learn to be a lady of the house. She vowed she really had no experience there, having scrupulously avoided domestic concerns these many years.

"We will see, my dear. It need not be decided now," Lady Alvinia acknowledged, grateful for Tonia's consideration.

And so, with great dispatch a letter was forwarded to Dunstable, the duke journeyed to Lincoln to procure a special license from the bishop, and plans were hastily drawn up for a grand celebration at the castle.

Alicia came to call, having learned that Derek had indeed put it to the touch and been happily accepted. She found Julia, Colin and Tonia relaxing on the terrace in the warm sunshine. "So, Antonia," she said, "you are to become a permanent resident."

"Yes, Alicia," Tonia replied. "I hope we are to be friends."

"Oh, I have no doubts about that," the baroness professed with a wave of her hand. And then with a wry grin she said, "I should have known what you were about when you read me a lecture."

"Well, I really couldn't have you making advances to my husband. It would have been quite insupportable," Tonia said mischievously, realizing that indeed unwittingly she *must* have been staking a claim that day.

Alicia gave an appreciative nod. "I understand your point of view, which you so effectively brought me to share," she allowed. "And to clarify *that* matter, I must tell you that I do hope you will not, in the future, feel disposed to charm *my* husband."

"Of course I will not, Alicia. I'm sure it will not be necessary," Tonia answered significantly.

Julia and Colin looked at each other in amusement, and Colin commented. "I can see you two are going to get along famously, as you understand each other so well. Though I don't expect it will always be clear sailing."

"Why, whatever do you mean, Colin?" Tonia demurred with a contrived innocence that made the four of them burst out laughing.

Derek returned from Lincoln the next afternoon, announcing in high spirits that he had handily accomplished his purpose. About this same time his groom arrived at the Radcliffe house in Dunstable. He delivered the message and announced that he had been instructed to wait for a reply.

As Matthew Radcliffe broke the ducal seal, he commented wistfully, "I do hope this is an invitation." He read the letter, which was signed Derek Neville, and Tonia's note, then smiled broadly as he handed them to his wife. "Antonia has obviously been up to her tricks again."

"Oh, dear,"·Mrs. Radcliffe murmured anxiously and began to read. "He wants to marry Tonia?" she said incredulously.

"Is going to, I believe he said," her husband corrected.

"Then—" and she hurriedly unfolded Tonia's note.

Dear Mama and Papa, I must tell you that I have been proven right to have waited so long to marry for I have truly found my love. It only just happens that he is a wealthy duke (though I have to admit I do not think it a bad thing). He seems regrettably short of patience and insists that we be married immediately. I do think we had best humour him. I am sure he has described the tentative arrangements, so I do hope it will not inconvenience you to come at once. Mama, will you look over our wardrobes to see if you can find a suitable wedding dress? Everything has worked out just beautifully. I will tell you all about it.

Love, Tonia.

"Oh, dear," Mrs. Radcliffe said again. "I suppose we must go, but I could wish it was not such a scrambling thing."

"My dear," her husband remarked knowingly, "Antonia has obviously offered the duke encouragement, and, considering the unhinged state of some gentlemen whom she did not encourage, I suspect we should take pity on the poor fellow."

"Matthew!" she scolded with a girlish giggle and left him chuckling as she went to inspect the wardrobes.

Five days later, the duke's carriage, which had been sent to Dunstable, pulled up in the castle yard. Derek was on hand to open the door, and he helped a small lady descend. He smiled engagingly as he said, "Mrs. Radcliffe, you cannot know how anxious I have been to meet you. I could not believe there was ever another Tonia, but I see I was wrong."

With an amused glance at her daughter, the lady replied with a charming naturalness, "Well, your grace, I admit to harbouring a rampant curiosity myself ever since we received your letter. I had begun to think Tonia would never find anyone to suit her."

With a grin the duke turned to the gentleman who had just alighted. "I am very pleased to meet you, sir. I have read several of your works and have been anticipating our meeting."

"No more than I, my boy," Mr. Radcliffe responded with a twinkling eye.

The new arrivals were escorted to the terrace where the rest of the household had gathered, and introductions were made all around. Presently Mr. and Mrs. Radcliffe were shown to their suite, though Julia and Tonia importuned their mother to come to them after she had rested a little so they might have a long talk.

"Did you bring a dress, Mama?" Tonia asked when they had settled themselves comfortably in Julia's room.

"Yes, my love. I thought the silver one that I said I would likely not wear would be appropriate."

"Oh, yes, Mama. That will be perfect!" Tonia approved, and then launched into a full account of the skirmishes that had led to this surprising outcome.

When dressing for the grand ball at which an auspicious announcement would be made, Tonia, in a flight of whimsey, decided to have her hair coiffed more formally. As she came down to meet the duke so they might greet his guests together, he looked at her in warm admiration. Taking her hand, he bent to kiss her, murmuring, "Very lovely, Tonia. And while I find it very seductive," he said as he let his eyes rest on the long curl that fell forward over her shoulder, "I think I prefer the squirrel's nest."

"How lucky for us both," she replied with relief. "I found sitting for this time-consuming handiwork extremely tedious."

He laughed and then situated them where they could welcome Alicia and the baron, who were the first arrivals. Over two hundred guests came to congratulate the happy couples, and all expressed their unqualified approval that the castle once again would be a family residence.

Halfway through the evening Derek purposefully waltzed Tonia out onto the terrace and then led her to a private spot in the garden. "I could not wait any longer to kiss you," he declared passionately as he crushed her to him. "Tonia," he admonished huskily, "I must warn you that I have discovered myself an excessively jealous man. I had the devil's own work to keep from assaulting John—and Robert, too. I did not like the way you kissed him, for I knew it wasn't the first time."

"But, my darling," Tonia protested defensively, "at twenty-nine I should never have been kissed?"

He had to laugh at her audacious parody of a gentleman's stock reply and admitted, "I suppose that would have been too much to expect, considering what a mischief you are. But no more, Tonia. Your kisses are reserved for me alone."

"Of course, Derek," she told him saucily. "I wonder you should mention it. But, my love," she demurred then, "you do believe in fair play, don't you?"

"Absolutely," he assured her. "I am addicted to it. I can't imagine you would doubt it. I don't expect to have any spare time, you know."

"Yes, I know," Tonia responded smugly. "I just thought it would not be seemly to remark on it" —an extremely imprudent provocation that once again invited the gentleman to behave most improperly, requiring Tonia to return to her room to have her hair redone before she could rejoin the company, having been demonstrably convinced that there was a great deal to be said for the "squirrel's nest."